I Will Not Go Quietly
True Stories of
People Who Refused to Quit

Covenant House
Christian Center

Table of Contents

INTRODUCTION

The stories in this book are true — they are about people who live in this community. They all have one thing in common: they beat the odds. They have all faced great adversity and sometimes near fatal circumstances. At the risk of their own humiliation and embarrassment, some have admitted their mistakes and indiscretions. Some have revealed the wrong done to them, having to relive the painful memories to tell their story. If you're like most, once you begin the first story, you won't be able to put the book down. These stories are amazing, incredible, compelling, riveting, encouraging, life changing and a must-read for anyone facing crisis or in need of hope.

*Note: Some names have been changed to protect identities.

Cast for Corrections
The Story of Tom McKinzie
Written by Richard Drebert

I leave home each morning to oversee child abusers, rapists, thieves and killers in a place where memories of past sins devour men like cancer in their cells. One inmate here dismembered his victim; another torched the "evidence" of his crime. Most offenders mingled with neighbors, family and friends for years until they unmasked their evil and *acted* out bitterness and self-hatred.

Because of their atrocities, these felons have forfeited what we sometimes take for granted living outside of prison walls: respect, freedom, self-worth, *hope*. Hammering on most inmates' empty souls is the same question that echoed in me as a boy: *Why?* Why was I born, and why had I tumbled into cruel hands? I was as bitter and hateful as any man I meet in corrections, but today I guide offenders to the Counselor who rescued me. No, I am not a prison chaplain or a pastor. I am a correctional lieutenant, and I could just as easily be telling you about my life from a prison cell.

Clug waits, a thick leg crossed over one knee, his prison slipper jiggling nervously in the air. Faded gang tattoos — grinning demons carved when he was 14 – ripple on his forearms as he tightens hammy fists. Bloody splotches, like two smashed mosquitoes, show a hasty shave on his knife-

I WILL NOT GO QUIETLY

scarred cheek, and under his breath he mentally paces off the room to kill a little prison time: 34 steps long by 16 paces across. It's a habit now, measuring boundaries: like in the room where he showers with a dozen other men; like in the Clorox-smelling chow hall; like in his own small cell that he shares with another inmate.

Suddenly, Clug's pasted-on prison sneer dissolves into a soft smile. Two children in hard black shoes and white socks with strands of dark hair dangling across runny noses clip-clop into the bright florescent-lit room. Between them is a disheveled woman, short, heavy and smiling wearily. She wears a tight blouse, and Clug's eyes devour her as she herds the two children to his steel table. He glances at the guard, who nods, and Clug stands to his feet. After three years in prison, the visiting rules weigh on Clug like a stone tablet.

Three seconds for a kiss and embrace.

No body contact except hands clasped across the table-top in full view of the prison guard.

But Clug is a thief today. He steals a few extra seconds in each embrace and hopes the guard doesn't notice.

None of the chairs score the floor as his children wiggle and squirm on their seats; all the furniture is bolted down in the sterile visiting room. Anger shows in Mama's face as she discusses finances, but Clug barely listens; instead he drinks in his babies' laughter and stores away each touch of their pudgy fingers to comfort him in his cell. He swipes at their snotty noses with a sleeve and chokes off a commotion inside as he glances about the room. He dare not appear weak, even in the company of his wife and babies.

Cast For Corrections

Clug started out as a petty thief before he was arrested for peddling drugs — one of several hundred files I might evaluate as a correctional lieutenant. And like him, I was a thief when I was a boy, too.

Violet's Prison

Church service ended, and in the small foyer, I crouched in the shadows waiting for my chance.

"You hit the nail on the head today, Pastor," a thin man holding a baby carrier said, shifting a crying child to his left hand and extending his right. The pastor shook his hand warmly and smiled at the woman in jeans beside her husband. She added a few dollars to the offering plate as the two backed through the double doors, and the pastor stood alone a moment looking after them. He yawned long and large, glanced at the bills fluttering in the offering plate perched on an oak stand near the church exit, then walked wearily into the sanctuary.

Section by section, the small Baptist church began losing light, and I scooped up the tithes, jamming the bills and coins into my pocket. A great pastoral sneeze sent me into a panic as I bounded out the door and down the steps, and the scripture carved into the base of the offering stand, "Give and it shall be given unto you..." skittered across my mind, chiding me. I piled into the backseat of the family car, where Dad and Violet waited with the motor running.

I Will Not Go Quietly

"Now listen, you get out here *right* after church is over. You hear? We been waitin' forever! Your sister came right out... just *what* were you doing in there?"

"Nothin'." I didn't look back at the little white church as Dad pulled away, and I slouched a little lower in my seat.

"Nothin' " was my standard reply to Violet whenever she probed — and it was *always* the wrong answer. I glanced at Dad in the rearview mirror, and as usual, he seemed to be driving somewhere in another country.

"Before I leave tonight, you got lots to do. I want that backyard mowed and..."

The coins felt cool in my fingers, and I rumpled the crisp bills in my pocket, dying to see if they were fives, tens or what. This morning I had stolen more than church tithes; I had stolen respect. I had stolen independence. This small triumph would console me a little when painful red welts grew on my back and legs sometime after midnight when Dad and Violet returned from partying. I glanced in the car mirror again, and this time I saw *me* with my practiced, unreadable frown. Not even Violet could know that I was thinking about where to get cigarettes.

Our tract house looked like every other on our street, with three bedrooms, fenced-in backyard and manicured lawn, but inside, our family was anything *but* tidy. When I was five, our father had wed a "prison warden" when he married our stepmother, Violet. We yearned to be with our older brother where he lived with our kindly grand-

Cast For Corrections

parents, but Dad had been awarded custody of my sister, Joann, and me after the divorce, and we stayed with him and Violet. My real mother lived close by, but we were seldom allowed to visit her.

After school, other kids on our street jumped bikes, hollered in water balloon fights, or scurried between houses with half-rolled sleeping bags, but my little sister and I knew our boundaries. Violet's "razor wire" rules had scored borders into our little hearts: *backyard fence, front lawn and driveway.* No one entered our exercise yard, and we dared not leave to dance in a water-filled gutter, or even retrieve a ball. From my earliest memory, Violet brandished control over my father and commanded his children with violence.

They could be a frightening team, Dad and Violet. Violet's influence on my father ran amuck when they drank late at local bars in our town of Clovis, California. Dad worked as a trucker by day. They called him Peewee, but he could flay with a belt like a man twice his size when drunk and goaded by Violet by night. I knew when the bars closed on the Clovis strip. I dozed fitfully until awakened by the creak of our front door, and then slurred voices scornfully tossed my name around the living room as Violet worked her manipulation.

Footfalls in my room. A pause. The jingle of a belt clasp and blankets snatched from my back...

"Out!"

I leaned submissively over my bed as the strap laced my legs, and I gave Dad his sobbing response. His strokes

I WILL NOT GO QUIETLY

were half-hearted tonight, and he stumbled out of my bedroom. I wiped my eyes and sat for a moment, foraging for nerve, and then Violet burst through the door. She was holding Dad's belt. Her flaming red hair was still bound after her night out, and her freckles, usually prominent, fled into her scowling red face. As she adjusted her dark-rimmed glasses, I fell across the bed, again burying my face and biting the covers. Her thoughts were shouting at me as she landed blows: *No good. Stupid...*

When my bedroom door slammed, I crawled into bed again, pulling the covers over my aching body to shut out the world. With my eyes squeezed hard, I imagined bare feet marching on our lawn — thump, thump, thump — and my welts continued throbbing until the marching faded and I drifted toward morning chores and elementary school.

Did the parents of other kids in our neighborhood tuck them in bed the way Dad and Violet did? Why did Violet hate me so? I was the same age as her boy. His sister and he had lived with us for a time until their father took them away. Did Violet hate them, too? Everything I said or did seemed to set off a riot inside Violet, and her verbal and physical abuse became as normal for me as brushing my teeth each morning.

My sister, Joann, and I worried together, schemed together and cried together, growing close as we wriggled under Violet's tweezers and microscope every waking hour at home. For years, I got the worst of the beatings until Joann reached her early teens — and started to fight

Cast For Corrections

back. Once Violet slapped her full in the face, and I expected Joann to leave the room crying, but instead, she doubled up her fist and swung a Sonny Liston clout to her jaw! I watched in horror as Violet wobbled a bit, then came to her senses and grabbed up a red high-heel shoe to use as a weapon. Joann turned to run, but Violet had her by the collar and in silent rage jammed the heel into her back over and over.

For just an instant, Joann's eyes met mine, and we seemed locked in a scene at the picture show when the film stuck in the projector. Nothing moved except that red shoe plunging up and down, then Violet flung a hateful look my way and stomped out of the room, leaving Joann in a heap.

"Why, why didn't you help me?" she stuttered through tears, and I didn't have an answer for a few seconds.

"You know why," I finally said. "I would have got it worse than you."

It was the first time Violet had resorted to using another object for a weapon other than a belt, and Joann and I knew that something inside her was changing for the worse.

"Tom, other kids don't get walloped like us. We gotta get away."

"And go where?"

"I dunno, but one of these days I'm goin'."

"I'll go too," I said, but then summer came around again. Violet paroled us to Grandma and Grandpa McKinzie's, where the very air we breathed changed from

I Will Not Go Quietly

the stench of bitterness to a sweet fragrance of Christian love — and livestock. Home would have been intolerable but for our summer respite each year at the McKinzie farm.

A Grand Parole

I never saw Grandpa carrying a gun or dressed in a police uniform, though he served as a deputy sheriff until he retired. His beat, Plenada, just 10 miles from Merced, included about 500 townsfolk in those days, and he never seemed troubled or stirred by his job. My grandparents, who were raising my older brother, welcomed Joann and me as cheerfully as their garden growing season, and we stayed with them until Violet and Dad uprooted us again each fall.

"We're butchering tomorrow, kids."

Grandpa's ruddy, bald head glistened with sweat as he eased his heavy frame into his recliner. "We'll do the rabbits first…"

Joann and I glanced at Grandma, who chuckled. At the mention of butchering, we both looked like we were sucking lemons. I figured that I was a pretty hardened farmhand: hoeing the garden, feeding livestock and even catching the chickens for Grandpa to wring their necks, *but his cute little bunnies sure got a raw deal.* Grandpa hung them by the heels and *whack!* At supper, I always blocked out the picture as I chewed fried rabbit.

CAST FOR CORRECTIONS

I left "the thief" at home with Violet whenever I visited my grandparents, busy instead following my older brother in the hayfields or swimming with my sister in a tepid canal full of pollywogs between chores. At day's end, Grandpa would sit us down and discuss our activities, while Grandma flumped on the couch in "her spot," which was imprinted in the sofa cushion. After Grandma broke her hip, Grandpa "retired" the outhouse behind the garage and installed indoor plumbing. I still recall the old farm kitchen and the sound of Grandma's hop-and-wobble promenade on the scuffed tongue-and-groove floor as she ambled back and forth, rolling out biscuit dough and frying up eggs and bacon. One side of Grandma seemed to have healed a little shorter than the other, but it barely slowed her down.

The safe, unhurried pace of life with my grandparents became a ritual of contentment that seeped into my soul, helping me survive my childhood. Each evening, Grandma unbound her long, gray hair that draped over the sofa cushions and onto the floor. With loving care, she taught Joann to braid her tresses as tightly as the bonds between her grandchildren and herself. I don't recall the scriptures she read from the big, black Bible, and it seldom left the wide arm of her couch, but the enduring portrait of her faith became a landmark for me.

In my grandparents' world, showing kindness was as natural as tilling their garden. How could they fathom the abhorrent life I led back home? I tried to tell them, but my world was incomprehensible. Their son, my father, would

I Will Not Go Quietly

never sanction abuse of their dear ones, and I shuttled between two realities with my brain twisted into the shape of a question mark. Where was Grandmother's all-powerful creator when Violet beat me? Grandma and Violet were as different as fried chicken and applesauce, yet each claimed to represent standards of right living. Violet demanded that I go to church every Sunday to learn rules, too. And where did this horrendous guilt come from when I considered my behavior of stealing, smoking and cursing?

Breakout

A year before Joann and I made our prison break to live with our real mother, our mutiny reached a climax when we devised a plan to make some money and ended up embarrassing Violet as a bonus. It had been easy to acquire a few blank checks from Violet's unguarded purse.

"The O needs more of a loop."

Joann studied my first attempt at matching Violet's signature, and I tried again.

"Perfect," I whispered, immersed in my crime. I definitely had a forger's eye.

"How much?" she asked, and I excitedly considered the amount we would steal from Violet this first time.

"Fifteen," I said, still chafing about lawn-mowing money Violet had stolen from me when I was younger. "It's enough for this first one." Our eyes met, and we both grinned.

Cast For Corrections

Joann cashed the check at a corner grocery store without a hitch, and the next week we forged another. But after our third "withdrawal" from the account, Violet cussed out the store manager and called the police. We took the haranguing by the authorities and were sentenced to a curfew for eight months, but it barely affected our spare lifestyle. The only freedom we usually enjoyed was at school, or when Dad and Violet left for the bars.

Joann finally ran away to live with my mother, and later, I joined her. Mom had remarried a good man who worked at Gobbler's Nob outside of Merced, and while I helped him milk cows in the early morning, Joann assisted Mom with farm chores before school. With free time at a nearby creek, I speared bullfrogs and Mom cooked frog legs and okra for supper, and we reveled in sleeping the night soundly without fear. No one abused us, and I had time to ponder my future for the first time. I decided that the day I turned 18, I would join the military.

Shaped Aboard Ship

"Son, you failed your test, but the Navy still wants you." The recruiter barely looked up as he shoved a waiver across his desk. Relieved, I signed enlistment papers and sat for a moment, picturing myself in a crisp new Navy uniform.

"Now what do I do?" I asked.

"Pack up, sailor — you're on the way to Chicago for boot camp." He pumped my arm a couple times, glancing past me at the waiting room, like he had just tossed another fish in his creel.

It was the winter of 1965, at the height of the Vietnam War, and the military needed every able-bodied man, with or without a high school diploma. I spent the next three months marching and shoveling snow not far from the Great Lakes, "training" for life aboard a Navy vessel. The Navy taught me to believe in myself for the first time, and even my appearance changed to shipshape, but painful welts still throbbed in my soul that no one, except me, knew were there.

I adapted well to the structured life aboard a tanker where the smell of diesel hung around my berth like stale cologne. Our vessel served the American fleet as a floating fuel station for destroyers and battleships. A few months later, I was flown to Clarke Air Force Base in the Philippines for duty aboard the USS Vesuvius. I was still a wide-eyed boy, rudderless and impressionable, as I squeezed into a crowded bus bound for the old ammo ship, Vesuvius, anchored in Subic Bay.

Awash in the chatter of small, brown-skinned passengers, I pressed my forehead against the window, enthralled with the jungle, the smells and the foreign culture. In the distance, I watched farmers plowing with water buffalo, not tractors. No one seemed to own a car, and the Filipinos carried burdens nearly as large as themselves on their heads or backs. Travelers trudged the same muddy, narrow thoroughfare as our bus, and there seemed to be no houses anywhere — no suburbs, no tract homes, no paved streets. Where did all these people live? *How* did they live? Men, women and children relieved themselves in ditches on the side of the road, unembarrassed, and drank out of muddy rivulets after the rain. I shook my head in amazement.

My mind drifted back, and I reevaluated my childhood in the extraordinary hue of this new experience. As a boy, I had felt caged and abused, but at least I had food, a bed and a roof over my head. A measure of gratitude took root in my heart — a feeling every bit as foreign as the islanders teeming around me — and for the first time, I discerned the touch of God's hand in my life. Yet, God still seemed distant, and at ports of call where the Vesuvius anchored, I followed my shipmates, drinking and carousing my way into their acceptance.

Aboard ship after duties, I played cards, smoked and read books. Sometimes burning questions about my past life prodded me to seek out the chaplain. He wasn't hard to find. We sailed in and out of Vietnamese waters, so the din of cannons sometimes echoed along the shoreline. Death was on all of our minds. Our chaplain was someone I could confide in, but he never pointed to the only one who had answers — Jesus Christ.

Warped Wedding

I loved Ella almost as much as her parents detested me. I was her father's worst nightmare: a carousing, worldly-

I WILL NOT GO QUIETLY

wise seaman who pursued his daughter. But Ella was in love — with my Navy uniform, with the excitement of my stories, with possibilities of children — and a part of her must have had feelings for me, too. My heart was twisted in knots at the thought of marrying beautiful Ella, and we headed for Mexico for a quick ceremony-of-sorts after just a few months. When everyone realized that they couldn't talk us out of starting our lives together, they prepared a traditional ceremony, and we legally wed. Pastor, Ella's family, my mother, her husband, my father and Violet were all there.

While delivering ammunition to a Marine division in Vietnam, I received a letter telling me that Ella would be delivering my firstborn. I barely made it home before the birth of my daughter, Deann. On my next tour off the coast of Vietnam, my wife wrote again to tell me she would be giving birth soon. "Hurry home!" she wrote. And somehow I arrived just before the birth of my son, Robert.

When my tour of duty with the Navy ended, we moved out of our little apartment in San Francisco and headed to Plenada. My hope was to plant my family in the rich kindness of my grandparents who had opened up their hearts once again. We stayed in Grandpa and Grandma's rental house on the same property as them, and it seemed a perfect start for us as I watched them doting on their great grandkids. If only my little ones could absorb some of that love that I remembered!

CAST FOR CORRECTIONS

My father had tapered off in his drinking and helped me get a job in the almond orchards for the Hershey Candy Company, where I worked for several months. But Ella was restless and despised the country life, and soon, we began to despise each other.

"I can't live this way, Tom! We can do better in Seattle."

"But everyone here has helped us, Ella. We'll break Grandpa and Grandma's hearts if we up and go now. Can't we wait awhile? We don't have the money to move anyway."

"I'm going, Tom — with or without you. Find a way."

Find a way. How? Violet stood over me again, and the welts in my heart throbbed as I read Ella's thoughts: *No good. Stupid.* An old bitterness welled up as I watched her slam the bedroom door. I reached into my shirt pocket, fingered my last payroll check from Hershey's and sat down at the kitchen table. $100 became $300, and I headed to the grocery store.

"Pack up. We'll go tonight," I told Ella when I returned with the cash. She seemed surprised, almost disappointed, and without a word to my grandparents, I threw our belongings and the kids into the car and sped out of town. This marked a low point in my life, one that would haunt me for decades. I imagined Grandma's pain as she clumped through the rooms of our vacant house, and I could never eat Hershey's chocolate without experiencing a twinge of fear. This wasn't kid's stuff anymore. Forging a check as an adult was a felony.

I Will Not Go Quietly

Even worse, I had unmasked the old Thomas McKinzie — the thief who acted out his revenge — and I hated myself for hurting the ones who loved me most.

Fables For Father

On the way to Seattle, we stopped in McArthur, California, to visit Ella's aunt and uncle and had been persuaded to stay. I landed a job managing a potato farm and worked long hours to catch up on bills. But as the months passed, my wife's depression deepened. One day, I arrived home to find that Ella and the kids had vanished, clothes, suitcases and all.

"Where's my wife?"

A distance wider than a hayfield suddenly gapped between Ella's aunt and me. "She left today while you were at work, Tom. She tried to kill herself, and her mom came and took her home."

"To Seattle?" I asked incredulously.

She didn't answer, and I knew the family blamed me when she said emphatically, "They said not to call and not to come after her or the kids."

Over the next few months, I withdrew into myself, feeling like the boy on pins and needles again, waiting for the next beating. I continued to work, and when my boss offered me a job managing a warehouse in Klamath Falls, Oregon, I moved immediately, happy for a change of scenery. I settled in, miserable but busy, until one day I received a call from Ella.

Cast For Corrections

"Tom, Deann and Robert are dying. They need to see you."

In stunned silence I tried to gather my wits, and I never did ask the right questions before hanging up the phone. The next day, I sold everything in my house, quit my job and found a flight to Seattle, while my brain twisted into that old question mark: *Why?*

I was down to less than $2 in my pocket by the time my cab pulled up to Ella's apartment, where I found that she did not live alone. Inside — where my two *healthy* kids bounced around like super balls — her live-in boyfriend drug himself out of the bedroom to answer the door.

"Oh, yeah, Ella said you'd be comin'."

With mixed emotions I gathered my children in my arms, examining them, hugging them and looking around for Ella, who suddenly materialized, looking smug. Her explanation left me speechless. Ella had divorced me months ago, telling the judge that I had deserted her and the children. Why had she lied about their illnesses?

She wanted me to come to Seattle and see for myself that she could live *just fine* without me.

Homeless But Hopeful

It was a surreal, intolerable arrangement; I slept on my ex-wife's couch while she and her boyfriend slept in the bedroom. I had forfeited what was left of my self-respect to be close to Deann and Robert — until Ella threw my belongings outside and had the police escort me away.

I WILL NOT GO QUIETLY

With no money, no friends, no job and no place to go, I wandered the streets of a Seattle suburb called White Center. I was now a homeless man, unraveling in my mind and hopeless.

Cold and hungry, I decided that getting arrested for vagrancy would be my best option to stay warm. I took to sleeping in a Laundromat on a folding table until a portly cop firmly told me to leave, but no arrest. The next night, I hid a bayonet in a deep pocket (it had been one of the few keepsakes from my father that I hauled to Washington), and when the same police officer woke me up and patted me down, he whistled a little as he pulled open my coat.

"Son, this is a concealed weapon. I could haul you downtown and book you on a felony for this."

I glanced outside where a cold rain blew against the Laundromat windows. I needed to be out of the cold with food in my belly where I could figure out what to do next, even if it was jail.

But to my astonishment, the officer handed the bayonet back to me. "I don't want to see you back here again. Understand?"

Was I still asleep? Did a Seattle policeman just give me back my "concealed weapon?" I jammed the bayonet back inside my coat and shuffled out the door past the police car where another officer eyed me suspiciously. This was the height of failure — I couldn't even get arrested! I found a church bus to sleep in for a time, and then walked to the Seattle-Tacoma International Airport, a complex where I could rest safely as I tried to locate a job.

Cast For Corrections

Lying on Ed Baker's couch, I had a home-cooked meal in my belly and could think clearly again. Ed worked for Alaska Airlines, and when I told him my story (as I dodged security guards) at Sea-Tac, he reached out to me in kindness, inviting me home until I got back on my feet. I signed up for classes at Seattle Community College on the GI Bill, and with my first $1,200 government check, I rented an apartment with an acquaintance and started a new life. I was a 23-year-old broken man with no trade, no family and no future. The college counselor placed me in a mechanics class because I couldn't decide on any other career path. I quickly adapted to college life, which was an institution like the military, with set programs to follow each day.

I latched onto a group of friends around White Center, young adults like me, trying to fill up the emptiness in their souls by drinking at honky-tonk bars. Partying filled up our space between classes, especially on weekends, and it never entered my head that I had fallen into the same destructive lifestyle as my dad and Violet.

My Betty

"Hey, Tom, I got a girl I want you to meet. Here's her number. Set it up for a double date," a friend of mine said one day as we walked into the college lunchroom. Dating had never been my strong suit, and I wondered if I could trust any woman again after my broken marriage, but I was lonely, so I called.

I Will Not Go Quietly

On the phone, Betty got right to the point. "So, what are you looking for in a woman?"

I tripped through a few standard answers like "someone with a good personality…" Then I got clever beyond my craft when I added, "and no one over 150 pounds…"

Betty punished me by letting silence hang on the line between us like stale dishrags. "Well, I'm *156* pounds," she finally said.

I swallowed hard, and then she laughed. "So, when do you want to pick me up?"

At a local honky-tonk, my prospects for dancing with this woman seemed as dim as the Hamm's Beer sign above the bar because so many offers came her way. I really liked Betty but felt that I didn't stand a chance for her attention. Inside, I was beaten down and felt unworthy of a relationship with a truehearted woman. But as all the cowboys drifted away to other bars, our time together actually turned into a date. And after a few more dates, I knew I was in love.

Betty brought new purpose into my life, and I rode my bicycle 30 miles one way after college three times a week to see her when I couldn't catch a ride. She loved the nightlife, and so did I, so we used up our free time hopping from bar to bar with friends. I moved into her house; and months later, we made a trip to her parents' home in Montana to be married. This time her family was in attendance, but none of my own. I graduated from college with a degree and new wife by my side but still carried the old

Cast For Corrections

baggage from an abusive childhood: self-hatred, bitterness and fear.

"Montana's too cold, Betty."

"California's too hot, Tom."

We weren't teenagers anymore, and our experiences had taught us that we needed to plan out our family's future rather than flit along with the winds of chance. It never occurred to us to ask God for guidance, but without a doubt, he was channeling our lives to a home in between extremes. Betty's aunt and uncle lived in Lewiston, Idaho, and the weather suited both of us — and God's plans.

An old sense of fear settled into my gut as I filled out applications for work in Lewiston. I remembered my "felony" in tampering with the Hershey's payroll check and worried that this lawbreaking incident might follow me to Idaho. The anxiety over authorities hauling me to jail perched like a demon in the back of my mind, tormenting me. (It wasn't until my father died years later that I found out that Dad had gone to Hershey's and paid off the extra $200 to keep me from being charged.)

In Lewiston, I broke into the filling station business, working my way up from mechanic to proud owner of a Phillips 66 service station. I had no experience in running a business, but I was determined to succeed. For nearly eight years, I sweated long hours — often wishing that I was just a grease monkey again — and then the poor local economy ate away my working capital. Without enough financial backing, I closed the shop for good and started looking for a job.

I Will Not Go Quietly

I found work at a giant department store, and my background as an entrepreneur landed me in a manager's position in several months. I settled into a steady work rhythm, feeling secure financially again, while Betty worked for Head Start. We planned for our first child, Daniel, then a year later our daughter, Cordi Leah. The bar life lost its luster when we stopped smoking during Betty's pregnancies, and we settled into a family life that was satisfying and stable.

Corrections

"I'm at the hospital, Betty. I injured my back. It looks like I won't be working for a while." I related the whole bizarre accident on the phone, how I had lifted a heavy piece of furniture that fell and pinned me against a steel pole.

After months off, I went back to work for the store, reassigned as a store checker. My days as a manager were over, and so was the overtime that kept our head above water. When I heard about the new Idaho Correctional Center in Orofino, I considered a drastic change in my career plans.

"What do you think?" I asked Betty.

"Well, I know Trish's husband is applying for the correctional academy."

"It's good money and benefits, but," I said a little chagrined, "you know me and tests."

Cast For Corrections

In February 1989, I graduated from the academy for the Idaho Department of Corrections as a fully trained correctional officer. For five years I served as a manager again, only this time, I managed the daily lives of inmates. I told them when to work, when to eat, when to sleep, what they could have in their possession and what they could not. It was like raising overgrown children, and for some reason, I thrived on helping these hardened criminals. I understood them and could have been one of them.

I thought back on how the police had never charged me in Clovis and Merced when I broke into houses and cars. I could still picture that cop handing back my father's wicked-looking bayonet, and I thought about all the years I looked over my shoulder, waiting for the cops to nail me for altering that Hershey's check (for no reason, since my father had covered for me). Any of these offenses on my permanent record would have kept me from a career as a correctional officer. I could have been sharing a cellblock with any one of these outlaws, but something or Someone had saved me from a serious brush with the law.

I still blamed God for the abuse he had allowed me to endure, but I had stopped asking *why*. Instead, I retreated into a silent, seething bitterness. When Violet died, I had promised to "piss on her grave" if I ever visited, and my relatives knew how I felt. Helping the inmates was therapeutic; I felt better about myself, but realized that I still had no answers for these men who might ask how to change. And I wondered if anything could heal me of a past that still haunted my dreams.

I Will Not Go Quietly

I was waiting, waiting for bad things to finally catch up to me again as they always seemed to in my past life. My wife loved me, my children were both on the honor roll, I had been promoted to sergeant at work, and I expected more advancement in pay and rank. Why did I feel so fearful and unfulfilled?

"I'll be back later. I'm going to church with Trish." A growing friendship had grown between Betty and the wife of my fellow correctional officer, but this church stuff annoyed me. I had never found comfort or answers in a church building.

I didn't see a sudden change in Betty, but a rebirth had taken place in her soul and a revolution in our relationship. Betty didn't argue with the old fire anymore; it was as if she didn't need to be "right" all the time. She cooked dinner for me, lovingly, and seemed more affectionate and *attracted* to me. I was confused.

One night while we watched television — a place where I could usually tune her out if things got too intense — Betty explained what had changed. "I accepted Jesus into my heart, Tom. I'm a new person. Inside."

Suddenly, I was *really* listening. Betty's face seemed to glow with love as she spoke about her new faith and how she wanted me to share it with her. "Come to church with me," she said, and I told her I would think about it.

Another month passed, and she asked me again. It was harder to refuse now that our relationship had become so comfortable. "I'm praying for you," she said good-naturedly. Two more months drifted by before I gave in.

Cast For Corrections

I stood beside Betty at Covenant House Christian Center, feeling like the only person in the sanctuary peering out a bean hole (the slot in a cell door, 4 inches by 11 inches). I longed to be standing on the other side of the cell door, free, like these Jesus worshipers, but wasn't it all a sham? I knew there was a God. I even talked to him to complain sometimes, but he never spoke back, or did he?

As the church service came to a close, I scanned my life, knowing that God had steered me past off ramps leading to ruin. Suddenly, this insight kicked open the cell door to my soul. It dawned on me that his intervention had always been gut-level and personal. He had been speaking to me through circumstances, calling me to admit my need for him. I had been asking the wrong question all my life: *Why?* I should have been asking *Who?* Who could take away my fear and guilt? Who could heal my bitterness and broken heart?

When I walked past all those Jesus worshipers to the front of the church to give my life to Christ, I knew how it felt for an inmate to experience freedom after 35 years of hard time. A weight lifted from my heart as I wept, and God filled me with peace for the first time in my life.

And my Betty was weeping, too.

I thought that I could never forgive Violet or my father for what they did to my sister and me. But Christ had set me free, and the old bitterness vanished when I told Jesus that I forgave them. Someday I will visit Violet's grave — I feel that I should — but the reason I'll go is different now.

I WILL NOT GO QUIETLY

I'll go to seal my pledge of forgiveness for a troubled woman.

After all these years, Betty and I still attend Covenant House Christian Center, where I am studying eldership courses to better serve the body of Christ. I'm pushing 60 now, a lieutenant at the Idaho Correctional Center and a grandfather to many of the men in my care. I realize that God has prepared me well for my work among the most hated in society, and though I shall retire soon, my heart will ever be with the man or woman who cries out "why?" because of a wounded heart.

I tell them about the counselor that can give them peace and freedom, and I say, "It's Jesus, that's *who*."

FORGIVEN AND RESTORED
THE STORY OF GENE NOAH
WRITTEN BY TONI HARVEY

I held my son in my arms and watched, as his body grew limp and quiet. I knew that I was to blame for his suffering. If only I could go back in time and change the past. I felt like my sins had come back to haunt me, and my son was paying the price.

"God, please," I cried, "please spare him the consequence of my sin. Lord, you know that if I could go back in time and change the way I lived my life, I would gladly do it to save him from this pain. If you are who you say you are, please, please, help him."

I was still praying when I heard a voice say, "It's time for me to take him now."

I opened my eyes to see an orderly in blue scrubs reaching out to take Kaleb from me. The red liquid that was given to him through the little medicine syringe had done its job. He was now still enough to perform the CT scan. Watching his body become so still and lifeless in my arms shook me to the core of my being. I began to sob uncontrollably, not so much because of fear, but because of regret. Why had I always thought only of myself? Would I have been so selfish if I had known what my son would have to go through as a result of the life I chose? All I wanted to do now was protect him. I didn't want to release him to this stranger, but I knew as big and strong as I was,

I WILL NOT GO QUIETLY

I had no power to help him now.

My wife, Jessica, put her arms around me, and we held onto one another and cried.

"Hasn't he been through enough?" I asked her. She knew what I meant. Kaleb had just turned 3 years old and already had a medical file two and a half inches thick. He had already dealt with tubes in his ears, clogged tear ducts that also required tubes, a constant runny nose, having his tonsils removed and living a generally miserable existence.

Refusing to give in to doubt and fear, Jessica took my hand and said, "Come on, Gene. Let's go back to the waiting room."

We gathered up our things and left the pre-op area where we had been waiting. It was the end of a long week, and we were tired. Just a few days ago, back in our hometown of Orofino, Idaho, Kaleb had become unusually sick, even for him. Our doctors told us, in medical terms that were impossible to understand, that Kaleb had a high level of spinal fluid and it was pushing his head apart. They said he needed a shunt with a valve put in to drain the fluid from his head. So we flew to Tacoma to stay with family and drove the rest of the way to Seattle Children's Hospital the next day. If the results of the CT scan showed what the doctors were expecting, Kaleb would be taken into emergency surgery.

The physical and emotional stress was beginning to take its toll. Jessica and I collapsed into a couple of chairs in the quietest waiting area we could find. She put her head on my shoulder and tried her best to sleep.

Forgiven and Restored

I looked around the small waiting area. The hospital had many small waiting rooms, and they were all set up to cater to children. They had games, toys and books. It was a lot like a preschool. As I looked around, I noticed pictures on the wall. One in particular caught my attention. It was a boy playing football. Something about the picture and the guilt and fatigue I felt made my mind drift to the past.

* * *

"No. Football is too rough and no son of mine is going to be involved in such a dangerous sport."

My mom refused to even listen to my plea to play football. It made perfect sense to me that since I was a 6-foot tall, 200-pound freshman, I would be a natural. But there was no arguing with her. So I thought I may not be a football hero, but I sure as heck can take any of them on if they want to go head to head with me. I was bigger and stronger than most of the other boys my age, and most everybody in my small community knew it. I wasn't afraid of a good fight and if truth be told, felt a certain amount of satisfaction knowing that I didn't have to take crap from anyone. Because I enjoyed a good fight, I never had a problem finding one. I quickly gained a reputation as a one-hit-wonder, and I was proud of it.

I really couldn't have cared less about school or anything associated with it. All I cared about was that I could take care of myself. I liked being in control. This was probably a characteristic that I picked up from my father.

I Will Not Go Quietly

He always taught me to be tough and to not let anyone mess with me.

Dad hung drywall for a living, and when he lost his work partner, he pulled me out of school many times to help him at work. I didn't care that I missed school, but I still liked getting together on the weekends to party with my friends. Since I grew up in the little town of Rocklin, California, it was inevitable that I would develop a taste for alcohol. Everyone that I knew had parents that drank, and we all started young, following their example.

Abusing alcohol eventually led to abusing and experimenting with all sorts of drugs. It wasn't long before I moved out of my parents' home and tried to make it on my own. I tried living in Sacramento with my sister for a while, but that didn't last long. When I was 18 years old, I moved back to Rocklin, but this time I moved in with my main drug suppliers.

* * *

Jessica raised her head, and her movement brought me back to the present. "Why don't you go get us some coffee?" she suggested.

I stood up and stretched before looking around for the nearest elevator. We had been in hospitals with Kaleb before, but each one was different and trying to find my way around the building always seemed to be a challenge.

There was no need to hurry, so I took my time walking the halls and thinking about things. It reminded me of the

Forgiven and Restored

first time I really thought seriously about my life.

* * *

I was going on my third week in the jail cell that I shared with about 40 other men. It was a nasty place even by my standards. The odor was a mixture of must, body odor and urine. To get from one side of the cell to the other, I had to step over the men who were passed out or sleeping on the floor. We had no access to outside light, so I had no idea if it was night or day. I had long since gotten bored of watching the other men fight and withdrew to my own little corner of the cell. I evaluated my life and wondered how at 18 years of age, I let it get this out of hand.

I thought about the events that brought me here. About one year before, I got my girlfriend pregnant and wanted to do the honorable thing, so we got married. I knew I was kidding myself to think we had lasting love, but I never expected to come home from work, walk into the bedroom and find my young wife with another man. Anger took over, and in one swift motion, I did a step-through on the man's knee and forced it to bend backwards. I had, in effect, crippled him for life.

I knew my marriage was over and had no desire to try and salvage it, so I left. I remember the coldness I felt in my heart as I listened to the man crying out in pain and my wife yelling after me. It had been so easy to hurt this man, and it gave me a certain amount of pleasure to know that I made him pay for crossing me.

I only walked a few blocks before I heard the sirens come up behind me. I was arrested for assault and battery. Unfortunately, this was not my last arrest. I knew I didn't want to spend my life in and out of jail, but I also knew that I wanted to be happy, and I was frustrated that I couldn't figure out how to make it happen.

When I got out of jail, I moved in again with my drug suppliers. It was an easy place to go back to. I was appreciated there. Everyone respected me because I could do things that intimidated other people. They gave me jobs transporting drugs or collecting accounts, and in return, I got my drugs for free.

A few of us guys lived together until I was about 22 years old. All I remember from those years is working and doing crank. I lived on a constant high. I did so much crank that I went from 220 pounds to 140 in a matter of months. I really never thought of my life being anything out of the ordinary while I was on drugs. When I wasn't high, I wasn't happy, so I stayed high. I assumed that's how other happy people lived as well.

When I turned 22, I met Lisa. She got me interested in martial arts, and I began taking Kempo classes and competing nationwide. For the next 14 years, my life became a series of working, competing, drinking and smoking pot. I finally felt like I had gotten myself together. I was living the American dream. I had a house, motorcycles, a job and money to spare. I couldn't understand why I still felt a void in my life.

Forgiven and Restored

Occasionally, my old roommates/drug suppliers would call me to help them collect on a job. Because I was given so many free drugs, it was impossible for me to say no to them. This created a problem for me and Lisa. The more I helped with drug deals, the more strained our relationship became. I also turned more and more to drugs again because I watched my mother suffer with cancer and refuse any kind of treatment.

My mother's life ended about the same time as my relationship with Lisa, so once again, I felt myself being drawn into my familiar world of drug distribution and collection. I can't explain the power that lifestyle had over me, but I felt powerless to break free from it.

* * *

I knew Jessica was probably wondering what was taking me so long to get back with the coffee, but I couldn't stop reliving the past. I sat down on a bench in the lobby and put my head in my hands. Somehow I felt that I needed to own up to what I had done. I had to take responsibility for my actions and beg for forgiveness. I was never one to extend mercy, so how could I expect it now? I didn't look up to see where the sound was coming from, but somewhere in the distance, I could hear a child crying and the sound was way too familiar.

I Will Not Go Quietly

* * *

My sidekick and I were driving through the slums of West Sacramento. It was a place you wouldn't even think of going to alone. As we got closer to our destination, we could hear the rap music blaring from the boom boxes that sat on the asphalt, while guys in muscle shirts with tattoos and do-rags worked out on their weight benches in the front lawn of this project community. Dogs barking and an occasional gunshot were also familiar sounds heard in this neighborhood.

We parked the car at the curb in front of a small house that was surrounded by a chain link fence. As we walked through the gate and up the sidewalk, I noticed the sheets that hung over the windows. The tricycle in the yard told me there were children here. As we got closer to the front door, we heard the noise of the television. We also heard voices talking, but our knock on the door brought no answer.

We came to collect $1,500, and we were not going to leave unsatisfied, so we did what we had to do: we kicked the door in and all chaos broke loose. Two small children sitting on the floor in front of the T.V. started screaming, while the three adults began cursing and yelling all kinds of obscenities. The stench of the crank they were smoking was overwhelming, especially mingled with the odor coming from the kitchen. Judging by the food and dishes that were piled in the sink and on the counter, I guessed it had been about three weeks since anyone had cleaned a dish.

Forgiven and Restored

All of a sudden, two men flew out of a side bedroom with pistols pointed and ready to fire. My martial arts training came in especially handy on jobs like this one. Kempo had become almost second nature to me by now, and I can't really say exactly what I did, but in a matter of seconds, I took one guy out. While I had him down, I took his gun in one hand and popped the shells out of it. At the same time, the other guy came at me so I jumped up, threw him against the wall and took his gun away from him. I began beating him with the butt of his own pistol until there was so much blood he was almost unrecognizable.

"Where's our money?" I demanded but got no response.

I picked up the television and tried again. "Give me what you owe us, now!" Still no response, so the T.V. went flying. It crashed on the other side of the room, and the children screamed hysterically.

I went over to the stereo and bellowed this time.

"I'm going to try one more time. Give me the money that you owe us, and we'll leave right now. If not, say goodbye to the stereo."

"We don't have any money to give you, please ..." begged one of the women.

I threw the stereo down. "Are you sure?" I demanded.

"Yes, yes. Please! We don't have anything to give you. What can we do? Please stop," the woman tried again.

"Get me the pink slip and the keys," I said.

"No, please..." the woman continued to beg.

I WILL NOT GO QUIETLY

I grabbed the bleeding man by the hair and forced him to sign the pink slip over to me and give me the keys. I'll never forget the screaming or the crying children as I left their home with the only thing of value they had left.

* * *

The memory was almost more than I could bear. I went into the nearest restroom and splashed water on my face to relieve the tension I was feeling. As I looked in the mirror, I tried to recognize the man who did those horrible things. The man looking back at me was not the same person who hurt people and made children cry.

"Lord, please forgive me for the horrible things I've done, and bring healing and restoration to the lives of those I've hurt." I prayed this silent prayer and left the men's room to go back and find my wife. I had forgotten about the coffee.

When I got back to the waiting room where I left Jessica, I found her sleeping. I sat across from her and watched her. I couldn't help but think how much she looked like an angel. That is what she is to me, my angel.

* * *

I met Jessica when my father remarried after my mother's death. During the early years of our relationship, I was occasionally pulled into the drug collection scene. Jessica put up with a lot, but finally one day, she said,

Forgiven and Restored

"Gene, have you ever considered going to counseling?"

"No," I told her. "But I'll go if you want me to."

The counselor basically told me that I needed to grow up and stop messing up my life. At first it made me angry, but deep down I knew he was right.

Shortly after this time, I told Jessica that I wanted to leave. I needed a change, and I wanted to break free from the world of drugs. I had a sister in Orofino, Idaho, and I told her I wanted to go there and make a new start. Jessica agreed, and so we packed our things and moved.

Jessica had been attending a church in California with her mother before we left, so when we got to Idaho, she wanted to find a church to attend there, too. It just so happened that there was a church right next door to the house that we moved into.

When we visited the church, we both prayed to ask Jesus to come into our lives. For me, it was more because I felt like it was something I was supposed to do; but thankfully for Jessica, it was a change of heart. She pursued a relationship with her Savior, while I went to church on Sunday and drank and smoked and did whatever else I wanted the rest of the week. Fortunately, she never stopped praying for me. She even continued to love me just the way I was.

It didn't take long before we began to feel like that church was not where we were supposed to be. We began asking around about churches and were told about a church nearby that had a great children's program.

The first time we walked through the doors of Covenant House Christian Center, we felt like we were home. We felt unconditional love not only from the pastor, but from everyone we met. It felt like a real family. I knew I could trust these people with the most precious thing in my life, my children.

Even though I felt a peace at the church, I still tried to keep myself at a safe distance. I wouldn't allow myself to be moved by the spirit or put myself in a vulnerable position with others. I went because my wife wanted me to go. During worship, I stared at the floor or thought about things I needed to do when I got home. I did anything I could to avoid being "taken in." Fortunately, Pastor Bear is a patient man who doesn't push. Even before I let myself get too involved with the church, Pastor Bear was always there for us. Every time we were at the hospital, he was there. He also called me many times just to check on me and see how I was doing.

It was in one particular Sunday service that we sang, "Open the eyes of my heart, Lord. Open the eyes of my heart. I want to see you. I want to see you..." and I finally got it. I was broken. I felt like God did exactly what I was asking him to do. He was opening my heart, and I finally let him in. The void I felt for so long was no longer there. It literally felt like the empty space in my heart, the thing I had tried so hard and so long to fill, was finally full, and I was overwhelmed by his presence in my life.

When I was told that we were going to have to take Kaleb to Seattle, I took him to the church in the middle of a fellowship night with two or three other churches. I was

Forgiven and Restored

broken and crying when I brought him in, and Pastor stopped what he was doing and called for the elders to come and pray. I knew there was nothing left for me to do now but trust the Lord.

* * *

Jessica opened her eyes and looked at me. "Where's the coffee?" she asked groggily.

"They were out," I told her.

We both saw the doctor at the same time. We stood to our feet and reached for each other's hands. We prepared ourselves for what we were about to hear.

"Mr. and Mrs. Noah," the doctor started. "I was here late last night reviewing Kaleb's file, and everything in it pointed to surgery. All I can say is either he grew out of his condition overnight, or there is a higher power at work here. I can't find anything wrong with your child."

My knees went weak, and I fell back into my chair. I couldn't stop myself from sobbing and crying out, "Thank you, God, oh, thank you." Not only did Kaleb receive his healing on that day, but I also received the thing I most needed from my Savior: forgiveness. Accepting the gift of forgiveness, and understanding that there's nothing I can do to earn it and that it comes by God's grace alone, has revolutionized my Christian walk. I know God is real, and I know he has a plan for us all.

I have not arrived, but at least I'm on my way. Not only has God forgiven me, but he has freed me of drug and alcohol addiction, and just three months ago, delivered me from the addiction of nicotine. I no longer even have a desire for cigarettes, drugs or alcohol.

While I am so very thankful for what the Lord has done in my life, I am even more grateful that my children are being raised in a church where the Holy Spirit is welcome and where they are being taught the unconditional love of Jesus. They will never have to experience a life void of his love.

THE CHOICE
THE STORY OF KELLY FINKE
WRITTEN BY MICHELLE CUTHRELL

It started with a dizzy feeling, but it quickly moved from dizzy to not okay, then from not okay to fearful and from fearful to panicky. All of a sudden, the voice on the other end of the office phone starting getting fuzzy, and I couldn't quite put together the query the young girl was posing.

"Heather, something is wrong with me — I have to go," I told my 16-year-old daughter, who was calling from a nearby town to request permission to stay out later to see a ball game.

"Mom!" she bellowed back. "You always do this to me! You're just trying to get off the phone so you don't have to deal with me."

I took a deep breath, grabbing a nearby desk to steady myself.

"Heather, I have to GO," I repeated.

"Mother!" she shrieked back. "Arrgh!" And then a dial tone.

I set the phone back on the receiver, stood up from my swivel chair and hoped that the change in position would stop the spinning. It didn't.

I shook my head, blinked my eyes and began to make my way forward out of the tiny office. As I stepped out into the larger room next door, pain like a gunshot pene-

I Will Not Go Quietly

trated my head, pierced my brain, and I felt an explosion, sharp like a razor blade, detonate inside my cerebrum. I grasped for something — anything — to steady myself. As I stumbled into Tammy's office next door, I could hear her ask if I was okay. We had known each other for years but had only worked together at the local school district office for two weeks.

No! I am not okay! Help! I wanted to belt at the top of my voice. *Please, help me!*

But the words never made it to my lips. Between the pain and the fall were the blurry surroundings of a stark white office as unconsciousness overwhelmed me.

* * *

The brain aneurysm that rattled my existence that gorgeous June day was an explosion that blew apart the rut that my life had fallen into. Beginning at least as far back as 1982, denial had become the status quo of my life.

Of course, everything looked polished on the outside. I had a wonderful husband and two little girls who loved me and cared for me. My family had just moved into a beautiful new home — a large split-level construction that sat one-third of the way up a mountain in a narrow river valley. Cozied up on the couch in my living room near our carousel fireplace, staring past the tongue-and-groove cedar through our sliding glass door to the valley below, my life seemed perfect. I worked a great job, and my husband even shared ownership of a profitable company — a suc-

THE CHOICE

cessful logging business that had been in the family for nearly three generations in our small town of Orofino, Idaho. We were the picture-perfect American family with our two children, our new home and our wonderful middle class existence. Except, of course, for the alcohol.

Corby and I were both drinkers even before we met. Every weekend was a party. We drank to get drunk, and we drank to get drunk every weekend.

During the time right after our daughters were born, we usually drank with another couple — friends of ours who spent most of their week out of town and who spent the weekends at our place. Nearly every weekend, Barbie and I would load up on wine and beer, and the four of us would shoot the night away playing Pinochle. The wine was the very best that the local convenience store had to offer, of course, and we could purchase it a gallon at a time so we would not run out. We would put the children to bed in the bedroom next to the kitchen, and the party would just begin.

Hand after hand, we'd bellow and shriek and laugh and drink some more as we played out each Pinochle game late into the night and finally, early into the morning. Our youngest daughter was only 3 months old at the time, and we'd often finish our drinking and card games only an hour or two before she woke up. Had my girls been older, I'm sure they would have wondered why Mom walked around in a zombie-like daze all weekend long.

Occasionally, we would join a group of friends and head to McCall for a weekend of skiing, which, of course, could not be fun without a good liquor-induced buzz. One time, the guys charged my friend Susie and me with the alcohol refills.

Like giddy school girls, the two of us giggled and teased as we loaded up our Voda bags with Schnapps at the bottom of the ski hill and jumped on the ski lift to meet the guys.

"I have an idea," I slurred, as I reached into the kidney-shaped pouch that hung around my neck and right arm like a purse, my legs dangling from the lift, sprinkling snow on the pine trees below.

I clumsily removed the lid on the pouch and brought the spout to my wind-chapped lips. Smiling at Susie, I indulged in a massive gulp. Her eyes twinkled as she removed her bag and followed my lead.

With the snow-covered mountain and the city of McCall as a backdrop below, the two of us finished both bags of Schnapps before we even reached the top of the ski hill.

"Watch out!" Susie bellowed, as we reached the peak of the mountain and the moving ski chairs swung around the curve to drop us off. "Jump, jump!" she yelled, but the alcohol slowed my reaction and by the time I pushed off the metal chair, I fell to the ground and rolled around face first in the crisp new snow.

My cheeks rosy red and my eyelids nearly frozen shut, I pushed up from my place in the freshly fallen snow and peered around to see my friend. I couldn't stop laughing as Susie stumbled to my side, offered a hand and helped

THE CHOICE

me up. Of course, she couldn't continue her assistance all the way back down the hill, where the two of us fell down and out of our skis every five or six feet from our drunkenness.

Sure, our adventures were crazy, and of course they left some bruises, but they were fun. We had fun. With friends like these and fun like that in a big, beautiful house with a family I loved, it seemed my life from the outside couldn't get any better.

On the inside, however, my life was an endless set of bad routines and habits that were pushing me away from the ones I loved most. Even though others thought I led the perfect life, I was just so sick and tired of being so sick and tired.

It was a warm summer day in 1985 when I decided that maybe, just maybe, I could do something about it. Something told me I'd find my answers in church. I'd attended as a child and been told about God and his son, Jesus. I had even prayed often as a child and into adolescence. But after losing my virginity at a very young age, I felt unworthy and rejected by God. From that point on, I kind of used God on an emergency-only basis.

On the day that I finally got the courage to show up at church, I did not know if he even cared about me. I believed that he did but did not know enough about him or the Bible to know if what I believed about him was true or just something that I believed because it was comfortable for me. But one thing I knew for certain was the fact that I needed something more fulfilling in my life than drunken laughs and mindless housekeeping tasks. There was a huge hole in my heart, and I had nothing to lose and everything to gain by taking a risk and seeking out God.

When I walked into the Sunday school room of a local Christian church and the lesson was "Sick and Tired of Being Sick and Tired," I knew that it was more than a coincidence that I was there.

After Sunday school, when the preacher began to deliver his message, it was as if he were prying open the door of my heart. The feelings of loneliness and emptiness that I had hidden so well were escaping, oozing from inside of me. I was embarrassed. It seemed as if everyone could suddenly see the hurt and the need in my life. The wall that I had so carefully erected was crumbling, and I was at a loss to stop it. I managed to maintain my composure through the service, but at the earliest opportunity, I practically ran out the door.

After getting out of the church and into my car, I felt an immediate need to cry. I just could not figure out why the urge was so overwhelming. I cried and cried and cried, and then cried more because I couldn't pinpoint exactly what it was that I was crying about.

"I must be crazy," I whispered to myself. "Everyone must think I'm crazy."

Once again I pulled myself together, started my car and began to drive. As I pulled away from the church, tissues in one hand and the steering wheel in the other, again I found myself sobbing uncontrollably and feeling so overwhelmed with this unfamiliar feeling of something more

The Choice

being out there. Sobbing hysterically, I drove across the old metal bridge that crosses the Clearwater River and onto the four-lane highway that leads to home. Without thinking, I found myself turning my car into the little Riverside Cemetery. I pulled my vehicle over to the edge of the little road that weaves gracefully through the carefully-manicured lawn. I'm not sure why I drove to the cemetery. Maybe it represented my sorrow. Maybe it represented my tears. Or maybe it represented something inside of me dying, so that something new could live.

"God," I whispered through sobs, "this is what I want. I want to give myself to you. I want to know you. Please, help me."

It's funny. People think death is an ugly experience. It's something they avoid all their lives — something they fight to the very end. But death to self, well, it can be such a beautiful thing. It wasn't that I physically died in the cemetery that day. But something within me died. And something new was born.

When I finally quit crying, I knew that something significant had happened to me. I was suddenly thrust into a new thought realm, one that was very foreign to me. I actually believed that things could be different in my life. Not only did I have the power to change my life, but I was excited and exhilarated by the chance to try. I left that cemetery feeling cleansed and enthusiastic about what my life would now become.

At that time, I stopped the drinking cold turkey. I no longer depended on the alcohol for my happiness, and I

I Will Not Go Quietly

was set free from the grip the substance had maintained on my life. (Later on in life, I was once again able to enjoy one or two drinks casually without the urge to get drunk or the need to drink to have fun.) That didn't mean I stopped partying and hanging out with our friends. It just meant that alcohol abuse was no longer my definition of a party. There was no more getting drunk and walking back in the front door sloshed, no more excuses to our two little girls about why Mommy smelled like alcohol or stayed out late on weekends.

There were no more worries about who would drive home after consuming too many beers; there was no more wondering about what I'd said and done that had been inappropriate the night before. It felt good, and I felt so free — so independent from something I had relied on for my weekend happiness nearly all my adult life.

Eventually, Corby began to attend church with me. He seemed to truly love the church, and our lives changed drastically for a time. Unfortunately, there were some problems in the church. We sought out a new one, but Corby eventually lost interest and quit going.

I continued to stay active in that new church for many years. I was happy there. I loved my church home. But over a long period of time, I began to feel an unexplainable need to seek something new.

There was a church near my house that I had known about for years and for some strange reason, I felt drawn to visit there. I had some reservations about visiting because it was a Pentecostal church. Over the years, I had

THE CHOICE

heard frightening stories about the odd things that take place in Pentecostal churches.

On the outside, Covenant House Christian Center was not much to look at — an old building with no modern adornments to draw the contemporary-type crowds who might seek such outward beauty. The downstairs carpets were shags of different colors, and the walls needed a fresh coat of paint. It appeared almost an orphan church of sorts. But something inside me drew me there, for no reason at all, and I knew I had to go.

One Sunday, I snuck ever so quietly up the front walk, past the creaking front doors and into the small foyer area that was separated from the sanctuary by two large swinging doors. The morning service had already begun. I could not see the crowd because the large wooden doors had been closed, but I could hear the pastor begin his message. I paused.

What am I doing here? I asked myself. *I love my church, I'm happy with my church — why am I here in a new one?*

A feeling of guilt overwhelmed me — the kind of guilt you feel when you tell your mother you're at a friend's house when you're really attending a rock concert she would never allow you to see. But for some reason, I stayed.

There in the foyer was an old wooden pew. I quietly tiptoed across the beaten, green carpet and brushed the dust off the orange crushed velvet upholstery before deciding to take a seat just outside the service area. With my

I Will Not Go Quietly

hands in my lap and my ears poised to listen, I concentrated ever so intently on the words that rumbled just past those intimidating wooden doors. I bowed my head, and I absorbed the words this pastor uttered as they echoed through the stillness of the foyer, and somehow, deep inside of me, I knew that Covenant House Christian Center was the place I needed to be.

I believe that different churches have different personalities and purposes. They all share the single purpose of equipping God's people, but the number of ways to fulfill that purpose is endless. I could see from the very beginning that God had some new lessons for me to learn at Covenant House. Some were simply reminders of things that I had learned previously, and others were entirely new to me. At Covenant House, I learned how to really listen to people instead of just waiting for them to quit talking so that I could speak. I learned how to be accountable to others for my actions and how to accept authority. And I was reminded on a daily basis to love and not criticize others. I was so excited by the changes I saw taking place in me, and I felt so at home.

I couldn't understand why my husband wouldn't want to be involved in a place that had shown such a potential to change me. Though we had a new church, a new pastor, a new place to call home and a new opportunity to attend together, Corby still refused. He had no desire to quit drinking or to change this life we'd been living so comfortably unhappy for so many years.

That, then, caused problems in our marriage.

The Choice

We fought because he wouldn't go to church, and we fought because he wouldn't quit drinking. His drinking became my excuse for a lousy marriage, and his failure to join me in my quest to serve God became the reason for growing bitterness in our home. I was resentful, I was critical and I was angry, and I found excuse after excuse to stay that way.

"The best thing about my life," I told him sadly during our last big fight, "is that I am not going to live forever."

Little did I know just how true that statement might be.

* * *

My head throbbed. Where was I?

Corby had beaten the ambulance to the office after Tammy had called and told him what had happened. He was gently massaging my temples, fearful of what was going on.

As I glanced around, everything looked shiny and white, and I could see that there were people in the office who wouldn't normally be there. Bright EMT uniforms glared in my line of vision as the rescue team quickly loaded me on a stretcher and rushed me to the ambulance waiting outside the office doors.

I fell in and out of consciousness as the ambulance rushed me to a hospital only two miles away. I fought for those seconds where I was aware of my surroundings, but everything just seemed so unfamiliar. Lights, sounds, gadgets, boards — a truck full of people talking in a language I didn't understand and using abbreviations I could only hope to learn in some other lifetime. I was confused, I was scared, and my head hurt so badly.

Out of nowhere, I began praying in a language all my own — something my pastor called "praying in tongues," and I reached out to God. This new way of praying was something that would have been so uncharacteristic just months ago.

"Lord, do what you want with me," I whispered softly.

And then, darkness once again.

***

The next time I awoke, a doctor was examining me in the Orofino hospital, taking my temperature and measuring my blood pressure. I was feeling much better, and I'd seen minor things like this happen a million times before.

"Doctor, I'm sure I just experienced low blood sugar or something to that effect," I told him, trying to dismiss my little office episode. I had a family at home I needed to return to and a part-time job I'd only held for two weeks. I needed to get on with my life and move past whatever had happened moments ago in that little white room.

"I don't think so," the doctor replied, listening to my heartbeat. After a few seconds, he picked up his pen and scribbled a memo on the paper tacked to his clipboard. "You are going to Lewiston."

Lewiston was a valley city of 32,000 people about an

THE CHOICE

hour from our small town of Orofino. They had a larger hospital and more sophisticated equipment that would allow doctors to take a better look at something that may only be a fainting episode, but looked to Dr. McGrath to be something seriously worse.

Medics moved me on a gurney from the hospital back into the ambulance. Another patient shared the ambulance with me, and I drifted in and out of consciousness as we headed to Lewiston. Even though the EMT who was in charge of caring for me went out of his way to make me feel comfortable, the ride seemed to take forever. I was confused and uncomfortable lying on what felt like a big board. Because the other patient was in the aisle of the ambulance, I was positioned off to the side. My head knew that our ambulance services were very good in town, but even so, my shaky, not-so-clear perception told me that I was just set up on a ledge — just out there, almost like extra baggage or an item someone forgot to put away.

The siren on the ambulance roared as we approached Lewiston, but as we drove closer, it was suddenly silenced.

"What are you doing?" my mother asked, somewhat irritated, from the passenger seat.

"I'm sorry, we can't blare sirens in this part of Lewiston. It's a law, ma'am," the driver replied very kindly. "But we'll be sure to get your daughter to the hospital as fast as we possibly can anyway."

I heard only pieces of my mother's disturbed response as I drifted in and out of consciousness.

The next thing I remember was the sound of the rub-

I Will Not Go Quietly

ber wheels rumbling against the cold hospital floor as cheerful nurses and attendants wheeled me to the CAT scan room in the Lewiston hospital. They put my mind so much at ease that this seemed no more serious than a simple preventative measure.

But when I finished my scan and they rolled me from the machine, the air in the room was visibly different. There were no more smiles, no more jokes. The atmosphere seemed heavy, and I watched as all the workers who had chuckled and laughed an hour earlier gazed at me with eyes of seriousness as thick as stone. The people who had seemed so personable and friendly only minutes before now turned into machines, mechanically performing their duties. Opening drawers, closing drawers, sanitizing utensils and avoiding my curious eyes. There was no small talk as they loaded me onto the gurney this time, and I began to fret as they wheeled me to my new hospital room. But again, darkness cloaked my eyes, and though I fought to stay conscious this time, I fell back into shadows.

***

"Kelly," the doctor spoke gently, placing one hand on my shoulder. "Kelly?"

I bolted awake to find the doctor's dark, concerned eyes penetrating mine as he leaned over my body. The doctor's tone was one of grave seriousness and concern.

"Kelly, you are a very sick girl," he began. I rubbed my eyes and took in the room. We weren't in the same place

The Choice

where medics had performed my scan.

"You have a ruptured aneurysm in your brain and you need surgery." I gazed up at him, not quite comprehending the words he had just uttered.

"You have a 50-50 chance," he nearly whispered, going on to explain that even if I did live, there would be a good chance that I would suffer severe disabilities.

He went on to share with me the severity of my brain condition — how it had affected me, and how it would continue to affect me if he did not perform surgery.

Given the seriousness of what he told me, I should have been terrified. I should have been screaming and crying and praying my last prayers and making my lists of the last 10 things I wanted to do before I died. But for some reason, I was calm — totally calm. I knew God was in control. My faith taught me that. My church had taught me that. And God had proven that to me, time and time again. With that knowledge in my heart, I was calm, and my husband gave the go-ahead for the surgery.

The next day, I wasn't just alive — I was perfect.

I was for a while, anyway.

Though the surgery had gone beautifully, I experienced complications called vasospasms that paralyzed the entire right side of my body. Doctors didn't know if it was a temporary or a permanent state. Fortunately for me, I really did not understand that I could not move one side of my body. My brain had been traumatized enough that I really wasn't comprehending reality.

But the paralysis wasn't the worst of it.

I Will Not Go Quietly

Each time my brain would spasm, I experienced a mini-stroke. If these spasms weren't stopped, the damage to my brain could become more severe and widespread. I could even die.

My husband had gone home after a long shift by my bedside when the doctors decided to send me to Seattle. They knew that with the severity of my situation, I needed a bigger hospital with more experienced doctors who could provide the care I needed to stop the spasms in my brain. With Corby at home, my mother accompanied me on the ride. God must have planned the timing because he knows how afraid my husband is to fly.

As medics wheeled me from the Lewiston hospital on a gurney once again, I couldn't help but feel that I was escaping death. Death had tried to steal me away, but I had won, I had escaped, and I was leaving. A sigh of relief filled my lungs, and as I released it into the warm Idaho air, I felt calm and comfortable.

When I arrived in Seattle, doctors quickly wheeled me into the emergency room, a very large room broken down into smaller areas by long linen curtains. Because vasospasms are a common complication after a brain aneurysm, the doctor in Lewiston had explained to my family that I may end up in Seattle needing a procedure called angioplasty to save my life. So when I arrived in Seattle, they were aware of my condition and were prepared to perform the procedure.

Doctors put me under anesthesia as they placed a balloon-type instrument through my groin, through my heart

THE CHOICE

and up into my brain and filled the balloon to open the closed blood vessels throughout.

When I woke up, I did not know where I was, and I didn't quite understand what was going on. I recognized that I was in a hospital but could not really remember why or how. There were people there — nurses and machines — and I had some questions to ask these people buzzing around my bed. I opened my mouth, but nothing came out. I tried again, almost gasping for air or noise or something to communicate with.

Nothing.

I gasped.

I'm trapped in my own body! I thought to myself. Tears welled in my eyes, and I panicked as I tried to run through my mind every possible form of communication known to man that didn't involve the voice.

Writing! I remembered. *I can write!*

Pencil! I motioned ferociously to the nurses in my room, scribbling my air pencil against a backdrop of charades paper. Seeing how panicked I appeared, the nurses grabbed paper and pencils quickly and rushed them to my side.

I remember thinking thoughts, forming words, telling myself that I would not remain trapped in my own body, that I would somehow break free and let the world know I was okay. But every time I tried to write something down, the only thing that appeared on the notepad was the letter C. Again I tried to write something, anything, to let them know I was there, I was fine, I was okay, but again and

I Will Not Go Quietly

again, scribbled C's kept appearing on my paper.

Sheer terror gripped my body. *I was trapped, and no one even knew it!* I thought to myself.

Overwhelmed by the thought and weakened by the surgery, I resigned myself to the thought and drifted off to sleep.

Sleep became a nearly constant state for the next two weeks of my stay in the Seattle hospital. Without a way to communicate or a brain that could effectively put together messages on paper, I felt useless, lost, alone. I couldn't sit up, and I was never away from the bed. I couldn't brush my teeth, I couldn't even eat. I was awake for such short periods of time that each moment felt like a disconnected piece of my life that followed yet another disconnect. Nothing went together, nothing felt right.

Until they took out the breathing tube.

The day doctors removed my breathing tube, I realized that I could indeed talk — it was just very difficult with a tube down my throat. The joy of realizing that communication is indeed possible, well, there's nothing like it. It didn't matter that my brain no longer sent the signal to my mouth and hand to say and write the words I knew I could think in my head. It didn't matter that my communication level was equal to that of a kindergartner. It didn't matter that most people looked at me as if I couldn't speak properly at all or talked down to me like I was a small child. I could speak. And after nearly a week without being able to do so, the other shortfalls seemed insignificant. I had my voice, and I had my God.

THE CHOICE

And my angels.

After I became a Christian, I had hung a sign in the entryway to our home that read, "He will give his angels charge of you." It comes from a passage in the Bible — Psalm 91:11. And after that aneurysm, I saw those angels everywhere I went.

My husband was one of those angels. I saw a side of him that I had not seen in many years. He was so caring and devoted. I saw things in him that I had never taken the time to appreciate because I was so caught up in finding things to criticize. He was so patient with me even though he was left to balance his responsibilities at work, which was in full swing during that time of year, and the household responsibilities of our two beautiful girls. And he did it all with his wife in a hospital bed eight hours away. He would travel the eight hours to Seattle to sit with a woman who could barely form sentences and then drive home to coordinate logging crews. He was amazing, and I was blessed.

I saw those angels in my daughters. They spent the next few months babysitting me. This was supposed to be the best time of their lives, and instead, they were stuck at home caring for a mother who could not remember her own phone number.

I saw an angel in my mother, who took two weeks off of work to be with me in the hospital. My Aunt Chris was an angel, having taken two weeks off of her life to stay by my mom's side. And my husband's family, who continued, for six months, to issue me my paycheck, even

I WILL NOT GO QUIETLY

though I was not capable of doing my bookkeeping job with the family logging company. And in my brother-in-law who, along with another friend, shaved their heads as a show of support to me because my head had been shaved for the surgery.

I saw those angels in the cards that I received from two friends who took it upon themselves to send a card in the mail every other day. We had not spent a lot of time together, but the two of them invested in me in a real way that touched me to my core. Their cards, as well as those from dozens of friends and family, brightened the lonely days in the hospital and reminded me that I was loved.

I saw an angel in the pastor of Covenant House Christian Center. Pastor Bear drove more than eight hours to sit by me, be with me, visit me and pray with me. One week, he even set up a special speaker phone so that I could listen to the service in Orofino from my hospital bed in Seattle. He followed my progress like a close family member might do. My new church family at Covenant House prayed for me daily and even brought my family meals after I returned home. Even my mother-in-law saw those angels, physically protecting me as I underwent the scariest surgeries of my life. The morning doctors were about to perform surgery in Lewiston, Mom was standing in her kitchen, staring out the window at the crisp blue sky. There was but one cloud in it — shaped like an angel. She took that as a sign that I would be okay. After the surgery in Lewiston, she stepped outside on the balcony to smoke a cigarette and spotted the identical cloud, and a peace

THE CHOICE

overcame her.

But even with the help of angels, recovery isn't an easy road. Especially not recovery from something as serious as a ruptured brain aneurysm.

Light pierced my eyes, and noise of any kind hurt my head. I experienced double vision, constant restlessness and no attention span whatsoever. I couldn't watch television because I could not focus my eyes, I couldn't listen to the radio because of the loud constant ringing in my ears. I laid — literally laid — in the hospital bed with nothing to do, nothing to love and only a growing list of things to hate about my new state.

Every day after the breathing tube had been removed, my nurses would walk into my room, hold up a yellow flashlight and ask me what it was.

"A banana!" I would exclaim with certainty.

"Kelly, try again," one would always nudge ever so gently.

"A banana!" I would repeat, frustrated that they would ask me such silly questions when I should be doing much more serious recovery work to get out of the hospital more quickly.

My mind knew that the object was a flashlight, but my short-circuited brain couldn't help but communicate the word banana.

I couldn't do anything for myself. I couldn't feed myself, I couldn't shower myself, I was not allowed to sit up because of the spasms — I probably couldn't have even dialed 911 in the case of an emergency. I was so helpless, so alone, and I just felt so isolated. I wanted out.

One day, I cried out to God. I felt desperate, destitute, abandoned and confused. Where was this God who I gave my life to back in the cemetery? Where was this God I had offered my life up to in the ambulance that fateful June day? I'd done everything he'd asked of me — I'd quit drinking, followed his rules, stayed with a husband who wouldn't attend church with me — where was he at? And how could he leave me like this, so alone, so afraid?

And then, in a moment so unreal that I often don't repeat it to acquaintances and strangers, I somehow separated from my body. Almost as if in response to my plea and in an instant's time, I was beamed to the stars. I was in the stars, and I could feel God. I could feel him so close, and he was just there — darkness and then bright stars, and I felt safe, secure and surrounded by love. I didn't even feel my body, just my mind.

It was a temporary experience, something I lived through only for a brief moment, but that short out-of-body experience provided enough love and security to get me through the really tough moments and remind me that God was indeed there, even when I didn't necessarily feel him. It was his message to me that he cared, that he loved me and that he, the creator of the stars, was in control. In that moment, that was more than enough for me.

The day doctors released me from the Seattle facility was a bittersweet day. It meant that I was healed enough to return to a home environment, but it also meant that I had to leave the cocoon of care I'd been under 24-7 at the hospital and return to an environment where I was used to being the caretaker.

It was Mom who always cooked the meals, Mom who always cleaned the dishes. It was Mom who always cleaned the house and Mom who ran the schedule for the girls. I didn't know how to be someone who did nothing — someone who laid in a vegetative state while her family cared for her completely.

When Corby was out logging, Megan and Heather had to babysit, and when they were in school, it was Corby's mother who had to come over.

Mom took me to physical therapy every single day. She showered me, dressed me, exercised with me, and when the morning was over, helped me into her pool for five or ten minutes — which was all I could bear — and then tucked me into bed for an afternoon nap. I couldn't work, I couldn't write, I couldn't listen. What did I do? What was my purpose? What was I living for?

One night, I found myself sitting on the cushiony carpet in the hall of my house, gripping the plastic bag of hair that the doctors had shaved before my surgery in Lewiston and softly crying over the life I once lived — the life that hair represented.

I'm worthless, I told God, over and over. *I'm a burden on my husband, I'm a burden on my children. This doesn't happen to me, God, not to people like me!*

Day after day, I would cry out to God — the same God I had dedicated myself to in the ambulance, the same God who had let me wander and play with the stars — and I would tell him that I couldn't do it, that I didn't believe, that I didn't feel him, that I didn't know why he would put me through this.

As people around me sacrificed to care for me, I would tell God how worthless I felt. As they fed me, I'd tell him what a burden I was. As they watched over me, cared for me and waited on me hand and foot, I would tell him how horrible this life was.

But one morning, when my mother-in-law was taking me to my physical therapy appointment, I told him something else.

"I am going to serve you. If I never feel you again, I am going to serve you," I whispered out loud.

That commitment made all the difference.

Eight years later, I have served God, and God has served me. Doctors told me I had a 50 percent chance of living, and if so, might endure paralysis and other stroke-related deficiencies for the rest of my life. Today, I walk, talk, breathe and write. I listen to music and work for a living. I interact with my family, play with my girls, name yellow flashlights by name and live the same kind of life I did before the aneurysm. My hair has grown back, my seizure medications are now gone, and I am a fully functional adult like I was the day the aneurysm burst. Through pain and trials, Corby and I have communicated and recovered, and I've learned to quit blaming my life's woes on him.

My healing is nothing short of a miracle. Even when I couldn't feel him, Jesus was there, holding my hand and

THE CHOICE

healing me all the way. Though he didn't heal me the way I imagined, he healed me in a holistic way. He continues to heal my marriage. He healed my body. He healed my life. He used my physical suffering to teach me something spiritually — that we have a choice. We have a choice to depend on God, when we feel him and when we don't, when we see him and when we don't, when we are dancing in the stars with him and when we're gazing up at those same stars, dying in a hospital bed. We have the choice, and when we choose to depend on him, that's when true healing can really begin.

NEVER ALONE
THE STORY OF KEVIN STOCKDILL
WRITTEN BY REBECCA WHITESEL

I was sitting at the foot of my wife's hospital bed, alone, as she slipped in and out of a coma. Nine IV bags hung by her side with tubes, drains and machines everywhere. The clock on the wall ticked away the minutes while the machines beeped and whirred. A nurse dressed in aqua scrubs came in every so often to check the apparatus, barely acknowledging my presence as she went about her duties. I was numb. I couldn't believe this was happening to us. Kathy, my wife, had just undergone a craniotomy for a massive, bleeding stroke. There I sat, breathless and disoriented.

Earlier that day, Kathy had awoken to a strange and nauseous sensation that she didn't understand. Her head was clouded, and her center of balance was off. As she pulled the covers back from her place in the bed and tried to stand up, she felt dizzy. Trying to steady herself, she stumbled into the bathroom and clutched the toilet to vomit. One side of her body went numb, and she fell unconscious on the cool bathroom floor.

***

This wasn't the first time my life had been confronted with a tragedy. Three years before, we lost our 10-year-old

I Will Not Go Quietly

son. Kathy called me at work, about quarter to five. It was October 10, 2001. Her voice was quivering, and I immediately sensed something was wrong.

"Brian has been hit by a van!" Kathy blurted out. He was riding his bicycle like he did on any other day and had been hit on the highway. She was sketchy on the details. "I have to get to Brian," she sobbed. "Hurry, Kevin, I'll meet you at the hospital!"

The 10-minute drive to the hospital seemed to take forever. Familiar landmarks seemed remotely strange. The world was a blur through my teary eyes. I took several deep breaths, trying to compose myself. I tried to talk myself into believing everything was going to be okay, that it was probably only a broken leg or something minor like that.

My mind was racing with thoughts of life with Brian; when we brought him home to meet his big sister, his first day of school, his first bike ride... He was just a kid — healthy and strong and active. Brian had his whole life ahead of him and would come through this. He had to come through this...

But when I rushed through the emergency department entrance, the look on the face of the nurse's aide who greeted me told a different story.

"Mr. Stockdill, come this way. Your son is in there." She was trying to be calm, but I could tell by the look on her face that Brian's injuries were severe. "They are still trying to resuscitate your boy," she stammered. I could see it in her eyes; the way they looked into mine then darted

NEVER ALONE

away told me she knew he wasn't going to make it.

After a few moments, the doctor exited the room and my eyes met his.

"He didn't make it," he responded as compassionately as he could.

My heart felt like it stopped.

"Can we go in and see him?" I asked, still in shock.

The doctor told us to give them a few minutes to clean him up first. Five minutes later, Kathy and I walked in to see our son's lifeless face peering back at us. I remember holding his lifeless hand — it was so cold. My world just felt like it stopped. Everyone could have been naked around me, and I wouldn't have noticed. All that mattered in that moment was that hand and that boy. I was in limbo, in a black hole that seemed to go on forever.

As I held his tiny hand, I just kept thinking, "This can't be happening."

But it was.

The miracles of modern medicine, the expert care of emergency medical technicians and the hospital staff had not been enough to save Brian's life. I felt crushed by a weight I'd never experienced before or since.

There is no greater pain than that of losing a child. He was part of Kathy and part of me. What would we ever do without our only son? He had so much life ahead of him! There would be no graduation ceremonies, no first love, no wedding and no grandchildren. There would be no more Brian.

I cried until I had no tears left. Kathy was in the same

emotional state I was, and we tried to comfort each other the best we could.

We were pretty new to Orofino, having moved from Seattle the previous year. We had no close friends yet, no church home. Oh, we knew some neighbors who had helped us settle in and get acquainted with the area, but there were no people we could call close friends. So we had to depend on each other.

Our daughter, Melissa, was three years older than Brian and was in shock and denial. She was 13 at the time of his death and struggling to come to terms with the grave tragedy. Kathy and I focused on making home life as normal as possible for her. She was entering her teen years, and we needed to be there for her.

Then three years later, tragedy struck our family again. Kathy suffered a stroke, an attack on her brain. She was only in her early 40s — isn't a stroke something that happens to older people?

Like the day Brian was struck, it began like any other normal day. I was at work and called home at about 11 a.m. There was no answer. But I knew Kathy was at home — we were going to have lunch together — so I called a couple more times. No answer.

That isn't like Kathy, I thought. I feared something was wrong, so I decided to just go home and find out what was going on.

I can't say I broke the speed limit driving home that day, but I did step on the gas. Something deep inside me just told me something was wrong. I had a strong connec-

Never Alone

tion with my wife, and my inner being just told me that something wasn't right.

"Honey? Kathy?" I yelled as I flung the front door open.

"Kevin," she answered in a faint, very slurred voice from the back of the house.

As I closed the door, I ran through the living room toward the part of the house where her voice was coming from. Our house is not huge, but I felt suddenly lost in its space, first glancing at the closed door to my daughter's room and then to the back hall as I searched for Kathy. The only sound was my heart pounding when I heard Kathy moan again.

She was lying naked on our bathroom floor and looked completely disheveled and very disoriented.

"Oh, no! Baby, what's happened?" I demanded to know.

She was conscious, but she didn't answer.

I put my hands under her arms and tried to lift her to her feet. But Kathy couldn't move her right side to help with the lift. And she couldn't stand up. One side was working, and one side seemed totally paralyzed. I tried again to help her stand up, but it wasn't working. She would slide back down every time I boosted her up. The strength she needed to stand was totally missing.

I raced to our bedroom, grabbed some of Kathy's clothes and quickly dressed her in the bathroom. She could tell by my speed that I thought something was wrong. I grabbed a kitchen chair and put her on it, and

I Will Not Go Quietly

then I leaned back the chair and drug her to the dining room by the phone.

"I'm going to dial 911," I told her.

She waved her hands in dismissal and answered back, slurring her speech. "Just put me in my recliner, and give me some coffee and a cigarette. I'll be fine."

"I don't think so," I replied, reaching for the phone.

My heart was pounding, and I could feel it racing as I pounded out the numbers 911.

"911, what's your emergency?" the voice on the other end asked.

"I think my wife had a stroke," I exclaimed into the receiver.

Just as I uttered those words, and out of the corner of my eye, I saw Kathy fall out of the chair I had propped her in. I needed help fast.

The lady at dispatch central knew just what questions to ask. She calmly directed the conversation quickly and efficiently to ascertain what the problem was and where the emergency was located.

"The ambulance is on its way," the lady assured me.

I clunked down the receiver and hurried to the place Kathy had fallen on the dining room floor. It was like half of her body wasn't functioning at all. The muscles on her right side were totally limp.

"Help is on the way," I told her. "They will know what to do." In retrospect, I think I was probably trying to reassure myself as well.

The waiting seemed like it took forever, even though it

Never Alone

was only five or six minutes.

"No, don't slide down again," I urged, lifting her gently and straightening her up on the chair the best that I could. I was scared but somehow felt in control to handle the situation. I just wished that this wasn't happening. My mind was filled with thoughts about what was to come. While we waited for the ambulance, I comforted her the best way I knew how.

After what seemed like an eternity, help arrived.

Medics in EMT uniforms lifted Kathy onto a stretcher, loaded her into the ambulance and took her to our local hospital. She was awake, but her speech was slurred, and some things she said didn't make much sense. Yet she was alert through all of it. Since Orofino is a small town of only 3,200, the closest hospital wasn't equipped for trauma emergencies. Doctors decided they needed to medically evacuate her to a larger hospital with more sophisticated equipment.

When the medevac team arrived in strange flight suits with loads of equipment and an oxygen tank they had to place between Kathy's legs, she became terrified. They had to strap her to a gurney and sedate her before they wheeled her to the helipad.

I was already racing to my car. I had to drive myself to the hospital, about an hour away. It might as well have been 10 hours. The journey seemed to take forever. By the time I got there, things had gone downhill quickly.

"Your wife has slipped into a coma and is unable to breathe on her own," a doctor explained. "We have to get her into surgery now." They were waiting for me because she was unconscious and couldn't sign permission for herself. They needed to remove fluid and take the pressure off her brain, and they needed to do it fast.

Before I could respond, the doctor walked me down the hallway and showed me the images of Kathy's CAT scan on the hospital wall. The entire left side of Kathy's brain was black. The whole left hemisphere was in blood.

I looked up at the doctor, took a deep breath and whispered, "Do what you need to do."

The doctor returned quickly to the room, and I stood there, in shock in the hallway. Someone handed me a bag — "biohazard" it said on the side of the bag. It contained my wife's beautiful hair.

"Do you want it?" the nurse asked. I didn't know what to think or how to reply to that.

"Oh, I, I guess," I responded. "What is this again?"

I didn't know what to think.

The nurse explained that they had shaved her head to perform the surgery. Minutes before the doctor had told me there was a 50-50 chance of survival. But now, holding a bag of lifeless hair in my hands, my hope faded. Now I was the helpless one. I put her life in the hands of Jesus. "Not my will, but yours be done," I prayed. It was the most difficult prayer I had ever uttered.

***

Finding Kathy on the bathroom floor that day, as unbelievable as it seemed, was all too real a scene to me. I had experienced something like this before. Like déjà vu in living color, my mind raced back to 1978, when I found my mom unconscious on the bathroom floor from a brain aneurysm. She died when I was only 19 years old.

I was angry. I cursed God. When my mom died, I turned and ran away from God even though I had been raised in a church.

As the years passed, I felt no joy. There was no satisfaction in my life. My job depressed me, and my family life was unfulfilling, although I loved both dearly.

I can remember several times asking God to just take me home. This turmoil of my spirit went on for a period of more than 23 years. Up to the time of Brian's accident, I felt like my life had crumbled. There was a period where I nearly lost everything I had. I lost my job, most all my possessions, my dreams and all hope of happiness. I nearly became homeless. I was at rock bottom, and I was dragging my wife and kids along with me. Still, I stubbornly refused to forgive God. The worse things got, the angrier at him I became.

After our move to Idaho, our lives and financial situation slowly began to improve. I thought finally we were heading in the right direction, but I still had no joy in my life. We merely existed, taking up space. I hated my life, and I felt cheated. Everybody else's life seemed so perfect compared to mine. I longed to experience life and enjoy it. There's a saying that life isn't measured in the breaths we take but by the moments that take our breath away. That's exactly what I wanted, for life to take my breath away— in a good way.

I felt like life had just passed me by, and I fell into a severe state of depression.

"God, end my miserable existence!" I cried out. That was the biggest mistake of my entire life. I thought things were bad before, but they were just about to get worse than I could ever imagine.

Instead of my life ending, the life of my 10-year-old son was taken, and I was spared to face the pain.

When my mother died, I ran from God, but when Brian died, I chose instead to run to God. My stubborn avoidance had gotten me nowhere. In darkness and despair, I cried out to the Lord. God heard my cries.

The day of Brian's death, a couple showed up at our doorstep just to be there for us. Pastor Don West and his wife, Kim, had heard about our loss and wanted to comfort us in our grief. It wasn't what they said that helped so much as their sincere effort to just listen and offer a shoulder to cry on if we had nothing to say. We went to their church the next week and have been friends with them ever since. Yes, God heard my cries and sent people who would become my church family. I am grateful to have Don and Kim in my life.

Sometimes church people say they are with you in spirit, they understand what you're going through, but because they don't know how to help in a time of crisis, they distance themselves. Don and Kim were not like that, even when I didn't want to talk about the things I was go-

Never Alone

ing through. They were just there for me.

It was at that church that I received God's love instead of giving blame, and it was a great comfort to me. It took me 23 years to come back, but now I was finally home. I've learned that God never wastes a hurt. God will use it to change our lives and to touch others, but only if we let him. He can only use our crisis if we say, "Yes, Lord," instead of asking, "Why, Lord?"

The three years that passed between Brian's accident and Kathy's stroke were years of growing in faith and service to God. My life had renewed purpose, and I grew closer to God each day. I believe that steady spiritual growth helped prepare me for what happened to Kathy. I had put all of my trust and faith in him, surrendering my will to his. I knew I needed to let go and trust in God, regardless of the outcome. God has his reasons, and I believed he would use the situation somehow.

After Kathy had the stroke, I felt helpless. I was in crisis, and I prayed harder than I had ever prayed in my life. Every morning, I got out of bed and saw my daughter off to school. After she caught the bus, I sat down to have a cup of coffee and wake up enough to make the 40-mile drive to the hospital. I used the time to talk to God. I was very open with my feelings and thoughts, and told the Lord just what I was going through even though I knew he already was aware of it. But the time on that drive provided quiet times, too, where I could just be silent and listen for whatever it was God wanted to tell me.

I started a journal after Kathy's stroke. I'd never kept

one before, and I found this to be the most helpful thing for me. It was helpful not only for recording what was happening and tracking Kathy's progress, but for describing my feelings when there was no person to express them to.

The days and weeks that followed Kathy's surgery were filled with anxious moments and hopeful signs. 10 days after my wife's stroke, I heard her say, "I love you." Though she spoke them in a hoarse, raspy tone because of the tubes that had just been removed from her throat, those were the three most beautiful words I had ever heard. Those three words melted me with pure joy and made my heart sing.

"This moment will be with me regardless of what the future has to bring," I wrote in my journal.

Two days later, Kathy said, "I'm hungry." She was still talking! Still, she wanted to sleep a lot. I looked at her lying there in that hospital bed, and she looked so peaceful as she slept. I knew recovery was going to take a long time.

"It will be a long process," I wrote in my journal, "but I have faith that the Lord will give her a total recovery and that she will somehow be even better than she was before."

Each day brought new faces into the intensive care unit and waiting room. Crisis touches so many lives. I wondered if they would allow God to move in their situations or if they were going through the pain on their own.

On the 15th day after my wife's hospitalization, I realized I had seen the ICU fill and empty twice since Kathy had been there, and she was still fighting for her life. There had been much improvement, and she would be moved down to progressive care.

Kathy was discharged from the hospital on the 28th day following her stroke. She was being admitted to a rehabilitation facility to work on regaining strength and the use of her right arm and leg. My health insurance plan would only cover 30 days, and she needed many months, possibly years, of rehab and therapy.

"I trust that the Lord will provide for our needs and that all will go according to the plan," I wrote in my brown leatherback journal, glancing up at her as I wrote.

Knowing that my insurance would soon run out and that Kathy was progressing very slowly had me disappointed and depressed by the 56th day. I had been hiding how I really felt from others because sharing that would make me feel naked and vulnerable.

On the 63rd day, I was forced by the system to take Kathy home in her disabled mental and physical state. She was physically crippled with the mental capabilities of a 2-year-old girl. She would cry hysterically and scream at the top of her lungs. It got harder to cope each day, and I found myself asking, "What do I have to live for? I have a lifetime of crisis ahead of me with no end in sight."

The financial situation was dire, too. They told me Kathy wouldn't qualify for Medicare until I had spent down half of my assets. Home care services were costly, and I didn't know how I was going to pay for her care.

Despite the torment, I chose to trust and believe in the Lord. I clung to a verse in Romans 6:3-5 that promised that trials help us to endure, and endurance develops character in us. Character strengthens our confident expectation of salvation, and this expectation will not disappoint us. For we know how dearly God loves us, because he has given us the Holy Spirit to fill our hearts with his love.

It's an uphill battle, and a crisis can take the wind right out of you. I tried hard to lean on the Lord's help by myself but learned not to go it alone. Church friends and family helped and that was good, but some forms of crisis require a professional crisis counselor.

I saw a professional counselor, and it forced me to open up and express all those things I was feeling inside. When I told him all the things I was doing to cope with the situation, he said, "Everything I was going to suggest you do you are already doing. I'm really amazed how much you've got it all together."

During those days in the hospital by Kathy's side, I wrote down some tips and things I learned that helped me keep my sanity when the world was crashing in on me. The journal was a major tool. Finding a quiet place to be alone with God and pray in the midst of all the chaos was another.

Just like there is a need to be alone, there is also a need to be surrounded by friends, loved ones and church family. I found I needed the support of others to lift me up and encourage me.

Reading is very comforting for me, and I chose to read insightful and spiritual material during those rough times. The Bible may have been my best choice. Not only did it

NEVER ALONE

take my mind off my troubles, but God's word filled my spirit and brought me hope. I could also share God's word with Kathy, believing that whatever mental and physical state she was in, hearing words of hope would be healing for her, too.

Taking in the beauty of God's creation was very soothing. I often took walks to collect my thoughts and soak in the beauty of the countryside. I began to find joy in small things, like a Mother's Day plant that hadn't flowered for six months and decided to bloom in the cold of winter; a sweet smell that filled the air from out of nowhere or even just snowflakes caught on my tongue.

Music soothes an aching heart and comforts a soul. I listened to and sang praise music in my car on the drives back and forth to the hospital.

I had to learn to open the flood gates and let the tears flow. When going through an emotional low in life, crying is a natural response and release. There are tears of joy and sadness. I had to learn not to worry about what other people would think, and just let the tears come.

I realized that it is natural to be in a state of disbelief. Can this really be happening? Many times I thought, "This can't be real," only to realize and admit, "Well, it is real." This is the stage of denial, and I realized the sooner I could move past that stage the better off I would be. Although once the denial was gone, anger was there to replace it, and that was followed by incredible sorrow. I learned it's all part of the natural grieving process. Healing begins in stages, and it's a wild roller coaster ride, so I'd tell anyone going through the process to hold on tight. When you finally feel a wave of peace come over you, you're on the road back to your life, but remember, it's a different life from what you had before.

Yes, life goes on. I now know it isn't wise to wish away one's problems. Trials are a part of life, and some are much harder than others. How a person chooses to handle trials makes all the difference. I chose not to be alone in my problems the way I did after my mom passed away. I chose to turn to God.

Now, I share my journey and encourage others to share theirs, too. We have a unique opportunity to use our experiences for the benefit of others. I realize now that someday a friend or loved one may be in a similar situation, and I will have the power to relate and minister to them. I can lead them down the road of healing because I have the map.

Two years later, I rejoice to report that mentally, Kathy is much better. She still cannot do much for herself physically — a nurse comes in while I am at work. Kathy goes to therapy three times a week. Each day does present challenges, but we know we can't do it alone, and we don't even attempt to. The Lord is our constant companion.

I can only see a couple pieces of the puzzle — God sees the bigger picture, and I believe that one day Kathy will be fully healed and restored.

It has been a long two years. Melissa has graduated from high school and is a freshman at college. She buries herself in her schoolwork, and I am thankful for the times

Never Alone

I get to spend with her. The pastor who drew us into the church that healed us is no longer the pastor there, but he still does prison ministry, and I help him out with that every Sunday evening. We now have a new pastor who cares and loves us just as much as the one who brought us back to the Lord.

I know with everything inside of me that there is a greater purpose for our suffering. God does give peace that passes all understanding. I know he will never leave me. He will never forsake me. When I am weak, he gives me his strength. He gave me peace in the midst of my storm. I encourage people to choose to let him do that for them, too.

Someday, when Kathy is fully healed, we will write a happy ending to this chapter of our lives together. Meanwhile, I am grateful for each and every day.

"Blessed is the man who perseveres under trial, because when he has stood the test, he will receive the crown of life that God has promised to those who love him." James 1:12

When All Is Stripped Away
Story of Maria Ward
Written by Angela Prusia

The tangled mess of twisted metal and shattered glass caught my attention. I stared at the newspaper picture in disbelief. The Suburban and the pickup were totaled. Surely, no one could have survived such a car accident. "How horrible," I mumbled. Talking was difficult with my jaw wired shut.

Silence replaced the small talk. A collective gasp rose from those seated around me in the family room at the rehabilitation hospital. I looked from one face to another. My husband stared at the ground, and my mom glanced at her fiancé.

"What?" I asked. I'd always been inquisitive — enough to drive my mother mad because I wouldn't let something go until I understood every detail — but this was the first time I'd asked about the accident that had happened two months earlier.

"We didn't want you to see that," my husband finally answered. He tried to divert my attention away from the front page of the newspaper.

"It's okay." My mother talked to my husband like I wasn't even there. "The doctors said that when she is ready to know what happened, she will ask questions, and we are to answer them. Remember?"

I clutched the newspaper, searching for more information. The words in the article — a jumble of black marks — swam before my eyes without meaning. I could no longer read.

"Who was in the accident?" I asked nonchalantly, as if I were asking about the weather.

My mother hesitated.

"You were, Maria." Her voice was a whisper.

"Did anybody die?" I inquired, glancing back down at the picture.

"Yes," my mother answered flatly.

"Who?" I asked, still as if asking whether we expected rain tomorrow.

"Andrew."

I paused.

"Was it my fault?" I looked up at my mother, who appeared to be trying her best to respond to my queries calmly.

"No, baby." She patted my hand, and that was the end of the discussion.

I glanced at the newspaper one more time, but it was as if I were looking at a storybook with pictures of someone else, not at the very incident that changed my life in a matter of seconds. And then I returned the newspaper to the table and didn't ask another question.

The absence of any feeling was a black hole in my life. The Maria I knew was gone. Among the injuries I sustained, the traumatic brain injury I received after being hit in the back of the head with a toolbox during the crash reduced my behaviors and knowledge to those of a child.

When All Is Stripped Away

Only a shadow remained of the woman I had once been.

***

My childhood was spent in the North Side of Pittsburgh, Pennsylvania, on the "wrong side of the tracks." My mother was a police officer in Homestead, a ghetto suburb of Pittsburgh. She tried her best to provide a comfortable life for my brother and me. If we lacked things, we didn't know about it. Plastic around the windows in our house kept the heat inside, and various rooms were always in a state of some repair, but home was home.

Mom sent my younger brother and me to Catholic school, and we attended mass each week, but largely, I ignored God. My biological father left early in my life, so I fell into the role of protector, especially when my mom encouraged me to watch out for my brother. I thrived on my "tough chick" reputation, even breaking someone's nose once. "Don't start the fight," Mom said more than once. "Just finish it."

When my mom remarried, though, I couldn't protect myself from my stepfather's sexual and physical abuse. Eventually, when I became a teenager, I could win the mental battles, but that only angered my stepfather more.

"Get out of my room," I said when he entered late one night. He didn't answer but continued to move toward my bed. I jumped out of bed and pushed him, but he pushed back. I ducked out of the room and ran into the living room.

I WILL NOT GO QUIETLY

"You will not touch me again!" I screamed at the top of my lungs. My mother woke up and came out into the living room to see what was happening. My stepfather looked at her innocently and shrugged his shoulders.

"I don't know what she's talking about," he said.

I sat down on the living room couch, sobbing, and my mother sat next to me. I looked at her and whispered in broken words, "He does too know what I'm talking about. He comes into my room at night." I glared at my stepfather, daring him to dispute my words. Instead, he picked up a glass coffee table and threw it at me. God was looking out for me because I walked away with only a scratch.

Our family moved to Florida when I was in upper elementary school because my stepfather was diagnosed with Hodgkin's disease. The doctors figured the warmer climate would help his condition. Mom was able to take an early retirement from her job because a stab wound in her arm had left the limb without function.

Mom wouldn't talk about what happened that night, but I imagined her in a hand-to-hand fight with some guy with a skull tattoo on his bicep. Mom was tough, so I could just see the surprise on the guy's face. He'd be so mad that a girl was beating him, anger would fuel him. That's when he would pull the knife and stab my mom. Blood would be all over, but Mom wouldn't even cry. I think I got my toughness from her.

A few weeks before our move, my grandfather watched my brother and me while Mom and my stepfather took a load to Florida. While we slept at night, our neighbor got

When All Is Stripped Away

drunk and crashed into the front of our house. Talk about a jolt. I woke up to a horrific boom and the smell of burning rubber. Not only did we escape the fire in the living room, I was able to help our neighbor out of his burning car. This strange event would foreshadow the ways God would use me in the future to rescue the lost and dying.

The move to Florida did not stop the abuse, and I learned at an early age that I wasn't to talk about it. Even my younger brother didn't understand the anguish I endured from my stepfather.

One sunny afternoon, we were in the kitchen where I stood at the sink washing the dishes. My brother, mother and I were laughing. My stepfather walked into the room, glanced at the jeans I was wearing, and said, "Those a little tight for you?" The mental battle began.

"Why do you notice?" I said. This simple question enraged him. He strode over to the sink, picked me up and dunked my head in the dirty dishwater, holding it there while I beat at him with my hands and feet to let me up so I could breath.

When he finally did, he laughed. "Maybe that'll cool you off," he said. My little brother thought it was a funny joke, but my mother and I saw no humor.

Once when I tried to report the abuse, I lost my courage. I lied to the psychologist who investigated my claim when she told me my stepfather could be arrested, and I visualized the heartache it would cause my mother. So, alcohol became my means to escape. I would sneak alcohol into school by using a plastic bag inside a Pringles can.

I Will Not Go Quietly

Lying also became a habit. I would binge for days, but because I excelled at academics and athletics, my problem with alcohol was largely ignored or unseen. I drove in a drunken stupor, and my friends and I were notorious for our reckless behavior.

I stood on the top of the car, the wind on my face. The car lurched forward as my friend pressed the accelerator to the floor. Now this was car surfing at its finest!

"One Mississippi, two Mississippi, three." I made it to ten seconds before my friend punched the brake. I flew off the car and landed in the grass, roaring with laughter at the adrenaline rush.

Even though I didn't recognize God's hand of protection on my life, he was there. Many times, I was an angel's breath away from dying from the many stunts that leave me shaking when I picture my own child in the same circumstances.

During parties, my friends and I would often drink ourselves into a stupor. At one party, someone slipped a drug into the drinks. I quickly sobered up to attend to several friends' needs, literally saving the life of one friend after she became violently ill. When the police appeared at the door, I had a "good enough" story, and they left us alone. God gave me the ability to be a protector, and he intended for me to use that gift for his purposes, but I was too busy using them for my own.

During my senior year in high school, my good friends, Jason and Robbie, both of whom were Christians who impressed me with their strong convictions, invited

When All Is Stripped Away

me to a Petra concert.

I met Jason in one of my classes, and we quickly became friends. I thought he was cool because of his jeep, but I see now that I was attracted to his strong convictions.

"Wow," I told Jason, as we stood among the crowd at the Petra concert. Hands were waving in the air around me. People were singing with smiles on their faces.

"Awesome, huh?" Jason asked me.

I nodded. I'd been to rock concerts before, but never a concert like this. "What kind of high are these people on?"

"Jesus." Jason's answer pierced my heart. The music swelled around me like ocean currents carrying me to my Savior.

"Jesus is waiting for you to say yes," one of the band members said. "Just confess your sins, and ask him into your heart. It's that simple."

I felt a tug to go forward to the altar, but I was too afraid of what people would think. I was a "tough chick" and not afraid of anything! If only I'd answered the call then. God waited for me, but I would have spared myself so much pain if only I'd listened.

During my senior year, my stepfather died. When everyone else returned to Pennsylvania to attend his funeral, I stayed in Florida.

"I don't understand you," my brother told me. "How can you miss Dad's funeral?"

I looked at him, wanting to tell him my reasons, but I couldn't.

"You care more about a stupid prom and your senior

trip than your own family." My brother looked like he wanted to spit on me.

Tears welled up in my eyes. I knew my family thought I was shallow, but I couldn't tell them the truth about the abuse. I continued to act as the protector over my family.

After I graduated, I joined the Army, largely to get a recruiter off my back. Since I lacked direction, I figured the training gave me something to do. After I finished my basic and advanced training, I partied hard because I had orders to leave for Korea. My boyfriend and I got a hotel room, and even though I heard a warning voice inside my head, I let the alcohol take over and had sex with him. I recognize now that the warning voice was God's, but I wasn't ready to listen to him yet. Once I'd given myself to my boyfriend, I found it easy to sleep with countless others in the years to come.

In Korea, I quickly gained the reputation as both an excellent truck driver and mechanic. I could drive anything from 18-wheelers to dump trucks and could drive better than anyone, including the Korean soldiers. Nothing intimidated me, not even unmarked goat trails or precarious switchbacks. Because of my skill, I was sent on more missions than anyone, including several dangerous assignments near the demilitarized zone between North and South Korea. The missions became so frequent, rumors started that I was sleeping with my platoon sergeant. Though the rumors weren't true, I was put in the supply room until things settled down. I excelled there as well, so I was promoted. Life was good — it was all about me.

When All Is Stripped Away

I loved to party. Not only did I drink, but I started taking acid. I figured I was being smart. Acid never showed up on urine tests like marijuana or other drugs, so I never got caught. I complained to a chaplain once that I was lonely, so he gave me a copy of the New Testament. I tried to read it, but I couldn't understand much. The Psalms and Proverbs comforted me, but I wasn't ready to believe the Bible was for me.

I decided to marry one of my drinking buddies. God tried to speak through my mother when she cautioned me against the marriage, but I wouldn't listen. My fiancé and I came back to the states to get married.

"Don't do this," a voice said.

I held my wedding dress close to me, covering my nakedness. "Who's there?"

The silence echoed around me. I was alone in the room. I shook my head, trying to clear the nervous jitters. I had to get married. It was too late to back out now. What would people think?

After a short honeymoon, I returned to finish my tour in Korea, while my new husband stayed in America. Marriage didn't fill the void inside of me, and the long distance only exaggerated my emptiness, so I slept around with other men. My husband didn't know I'd been unfaithful, so when I finished my tour, he was ready for me to move home with him to Idaho. Soon I became pregnant with our son.

My husband's parents were believers in Jesus Christ, so they started talking to me about Jesus. I didn't want to listen, but they wouldn't stop. I finally agreed to go to church with them just to get them off my back. They arranged for me to talk with a woman who was a really devoted Catholic, so I went to her house and spent the afternoon with her. Everything she said made logical sense, so I decided to pray the sinner's prayer — a prayer you pray to Jesus that affirms that you are a person who makes mistakes, and that you want to accept Christ as your personal savior so that you can receive forgiveness from those mistakes and live with God in heaven forever.

But like with everything else in my life, I put faith in myself. I longed for approval, and I wanted to excel, so I tried to become the model Christian. I wasn't ready to give up the bar scene, so I repented on Sunday for my mistakes on Friday and Saturday. I went through the motions and fell in step with the traditions. I got good at prayer and even joined the choir. I couldn't even sing, but I was great at showmanship. I'm one of those rare people who love to get in front of people.

My husband had little ambition, but he was easy to ignore. My young son kept me busy as did my job as a paralegal. I got lots of pats on the back from people. I was a Little League coach, I excelled at my job, and my son was doing well in school and in sports. What I didn't understand then was how much I really lacked in my life. I might've understood Jesus in my head, but I'd never let him inside my heart.

When I got hired with the Idaho Department of Labor (Job Services), I found the same sense of camaraderie I'd had in the Army. My coworkers became family. Andrew was the father I never had, a dapper gentleman with a huge heart. He took me under his wing. Whenever one of my clients became angry — often burly guys who'd been dislocated from the timber industry — Andrew would take on a protective role. He wasn't a big man, but his voice was authoritative.

A guy who reminded me of the Hulk hovered over my desk screaming obscenities at me. He reeked of alcohol.

"Everything okay, Maria?" Andrew came out of his office.

The man snarled at Andrew.

"We're here to help you, sir," Andrew said, his voice calm.

The Hulk towered over Andrew. I cringed, sure he'd pound Andrew to a pulp. The two eyed one another, coming to a silent agreement.

"Sit down," Andrew commanded, and the guy obeyed like a puppy that had been scolded. "And Maria will help you." Andrew winked at me as he turned toward his office.

My boss, Joseph, was a veteran, so we had an instant bond. He was easy to work for because of the warm climate he created in the office. Prue was everyone's mother. She never had a bad word to say about anyone. Jasmine was the life of the party. We were close in age with young children, so we were good friends.

The five of us were together that June night in 1998, when we were hit head on by the drunk driver in the pickup. I have no recollection of the accident, so others

I Will Not Go Quietly

have filled in the details. We'd gone to an awards ceremony in Lewistown, about an hour's drive from Orofino. The only memory I have is the laughter the five of us shared together.

"Move over," Andrew said. He got in the driver's seat and pushed Jasmine to the middle seat.

"Why?" Jasmine complained.

"Because you've been drinking." Andrew glanced at the rest of us. "You all have."

Witnesses say we stopped at Dairy Queen to get an ice cream cake for Jasmine's husband's birthday, but I remember nothing. Less than 15 miles later, we were hit head on by a pickup.

The accident report said the pickup driver and his passenger were racing another vehicle at speeds between 100-120 miles per hour. When the pickup swerved into our lane to pass an 18-wheeler, Andrew had no time to react. The engine in the Suburban was shoved into the front seat, killing Andrew instantly. Jasmine died a few minutes later. Prue's pelvis was crushed, and Joseph suffered an open head wound. A toolbox slammed into the back of my head, damaging my brain. Both the driver and the passenger in the pickup were killed.

I can only imagine the details of the moment that altered my life. The horror on Andrew's face in that split second he saw the pickup... the deafening sound of our vehicles slamming into one another... the flash of the emergency lights... the muffled voices on the radios... the bodies lying on the ground. Why did God spare me?

When All Is Stripped Away

I was air-flighted to Spokane, Washington, where I underwent heart surgery at Sacred Heart Medical Center. The fact that I was alive was nothing short of a miracle. Later in the therapy room, one of my doctors shook my hand in amazement; he'd never seen someone with a torn aorta survive. I suffered from a collapsed lung and damage to my liver and spleen. My jaw also needed to be rebuilt. There were other injuries too numerous to mention that I just can't remember after the trauma I experienced.

When I look at my response to Andrew's death, I marvel at my detachment, even though I understand the reason. My brain had to protect itself. I couldn't handle the emotional trauma on top of the physical damage I'd suffered. The blow to the back of my head and subsequent swelling of my brain was so severe, my head turned black in color.

After the surgeries, I spent months in an inpatient rehabilitation hospital relearning everything. I didn't know how to walk or how to lift my legs when I climbed stairs. I had to learn to read again. I couldn't remember how to hold a pencil or how to swallow. Memories had to be recreated. I couldn't remember that I'd been on the swim team in high school or that I'd graduated in the top 10 percent of my large class. My life was an endless series of therapy — physical therapy, occupational therapy and speech therapy.

I learned relatively fast, but everything had to be reintroduced to me. I couldn't understand my limitations, so I was easily frustrated. I threw tantrums like a toddler would. Once when my 5-year-old son came to see me, I threw a major fit because I wanted to play, but I couldn't because of my physical limitations.

I left the hospital about six months after my accident. Even though my mom argued against my release, I told the doctors I was ready. I should've stayed in the hospital. I was ill-prepared for the reality of living with a traumatic brain injury. Nothing was easy.

My husband worked nights, so he was too tired during the day to take me to my countless doctor and therapy appointments. I could no longer be the caregiver for our son or the person who handled the finances and everyday tasks of managing a household, and that frustrated both of us. Since I couldn't drive, I found rides with a manipulative man who pretended to be my friend. Because of the void in my life, I began to sleep with him. When I tried to break things off, the man began to stalk me. Things got so bad, I obtained a concealed weapons permit. Though he was eventually prosecuted, my marriage was over. My husband and I soon divorced.

I quit going to church altogether because I was too uncomfortable going to the same place as my ex-in-laws. Refusing to admit my limitations, I applied for a management position with Job Services. When I didn't get the job, I was crushed. I'd excelled at everything I'd ever done. Now my life was nothing but failure. I had nowhere else to turn when a friend invited me to Covenant House Christian Center. I finally found what I'd been missing.

Pastor Tristan "Bear" Harvey preached a message that

When All Is Stripped Away

cut right to my heart. I responded to the altar call and broke down like never before. I lay down on the altar sobbing my heart out. Despite my embarrassment, I couldn't move. When I finally turned around, the entire congregation stared at me. I looked at Pastor Bear, and he held out his arms. "Come here, angel," he said. I sank into his embrace, feeling like the prodigal son, or in this case, daughter. I belonged here. I'd finally come home.

The accident left me lost and alone, but the spirit of God had me right where he wanted. I had to rely on God. I couldn't credit myself for anything. This time I understood the sinner's prayer in my heart. I was overwhelmed that the God of the universe would die for me. I began to experience the power of prayer. Scripture opened up, and God's spirit pierced my heart.

I knew I had a lot of changes to make in my life. The first was my addiction to alcohol.

"I'm having a 'pouring out' party," I said to Pastor on the phone one day.

"A what?"

"A 'pouring out' party," I repeated, a smile in my voice. "Come over."

Curiosity got the better of Pastor and his wife. They were at my apartment within minutes.

"Look at me," Pastor's wife said, as she held up a beer in her hand. "You don't see this every day."

A fit of laughter hit the three of us as we poured bottle after bottle down the drain. I couldn't remember the last time I'd had so much fun.

I Will Not Go Quietly

I took a six pack and flushed the beer down the toilet.

"How much money do you figure just hit the sewer?" Pastor asked.

"Probably hundreds," I laughed. What a picture of Christ's power in my life. The alcohol — like my sin — poured out of me so Jesus could fill me up. Praise God, I haven't had a drink since that night.

God has brought me full circle. I'm taking Bible classes through correspondence and taking classes to earn my degree in social work. I have a full-time job as a resource and services coordinator, helping people with needs navigate the bureaucratic systems in the service industry and creating resources and services that are needed but absent in the community. I'm also the Youth Pastor at church and loving it.

In ministering to youth, God is bringing back the innocence I lost because of the abuse in my life. God is using me to build relationships with the young people in our church. My prayer is that I can stop someone from making the same mistakes I did. I challenge the youth to listen to God. He is calling to us all the time. If only we'll listen, we'd be spared so much pain.

Pastor Bear and his wife welcomed me and my son into their family. Often, they'd stop by just to see how I was doing. Friendship also came from within the church.

I wasn't looking for marriage when I met my husband, Doug. Pastor Bear teased me about my time on the Internet, so I was embarrassed to tell him I'd met Doug in an Internet chat room. Pastor had his concerns at first, but

When All Is Stripped Away

God's hand was so apparent, even Pastor was surprised.

Orofino is not a big town, so when I learned that the person I'd been corresponding with on the Internet was someone who lived in the same town, I was shocked. I had some high expectations, and Doug filled them all. You see, I had prerequisites for any man I was going to allow in my life. My future husband had to be a Christian. I didn't want to marry someone who'd been married before, and I didn't want a man with children. Since I love the outdoors, I also wanted someone with the same love. These requirements alone seemed pretty impossible, especially in a small town with a population of only about 4,000. So when God sent Doug, I was amazed.

On top of everything else, Doug was a physical therapist assistant — the perfect occupation for someone with a traumatic brain injury and continuing physical ailments. As a friend said, I couldn't have found a better husband. Doug accepts me for who I am and is very patient with my eccentricities, often laughing with me and others about silly things I've done or said. He is never hurtful or jealous of the time I spend ministering to others. Even though youth ministry is not Doug's passion, he is often helpful and always prayerful. Since God blessed Doug with an incredible talent to play the drums, he is also encouraging me to participate once again in the music ministry so we can serve side by side.

Being a survivor makes me wonder about the plans God has for me. I survived abuse, alcoholism, slanderous hatred and countless near-death experiences. When I was undergoing therapy, one of my evaluators made the comment that I must've been a genius before my accident because my scores afterward were so normal. God alone gets the credit for healing me — both inside and out. Without him, I wouldn't be the woman I am today.

Recently, a woman at church told me how God created me to be a warrior-soldier for him. At first, I was confused. The words seemed to be synonymous until I gave the subject more thought. Two distinct word pictures began to emerge.

A warrior is one who is engaged or experienced in battle, often leading the troops to battle. A soldier is one who serves — a loyal follower — willing to fight side by side with other soldiers. My favorite verses in the Bible are in the book of Ephesians when Paul talks about the armor of God. For so much of my life, I fought the devil with my own strength. But I can't win on my own. To be victorious, I need to "be strong in the Lord and in his mighty power." Paul writes, "Put on the full armor of God so that you can take your stand against the devil's schemes. For our struggle is not against flesh and blood, but against the rulers, against the authorities, against the powers of this dark world and against the spiritual forces of evil in the heavenly realms... Stand firm then, with the belt of truth buckled around your waist, with the breastplate of righteousness... the gospel of peace... take up the shield of faith... take the helmet of salvation, and the sword of the Spirit... and pray." Only then can I be a warrior for God, leading the troops, or be a soldier for God, fighting along-

When All Is Stripped Away

side of them.

Before I gave my life to Christ, I kept busy to fill something within me. Now I keep busy because God has called me to serve. When I look at the gifts he's given me and the strength he's empowered me with to overcome so much in my life, I know he wants me to use what I've learned to serve others. This is especially true in the area of youth ministry because I can identify with the struggles teenagers face.

Knowing God in our heads is not enough. We have to know him in our hearts. I tell the youth at Covenant House Christian Center that we're all just people — we're going to mess up — but Jesus loved us enough to die for us. His death gives us power not only to live with him in heaven forever, but also to save us from ourselves while we are here on this earth. We don't have to be condemned for our sins. My sin is worthy of death, but God is mercy. I'm so ashamed of the life I once lived. I should have embraced Jesus, but I wanted control. Ironically, though, I never was in control. Sin controlled me. What a privilege to have a second chance.

God would never harm me. The accident wasn't from him. Rather, the accident was the consequence of sin. Through the accident, he stepped down to earth to pick me up out of my mistakes and save me. That's the heart knowledge that I didn't understand when I tried to approach Jesus Christ through logic. Without heart knowledge, I didn't really know Jesus. Without Covenant House, I may never have learned the heart knowledge and would

I Will Not Go Quietly

still be lost and searching to fill the void in my life that only Jesus Christ can fill.

The accident stripped me of everything — my identity, my abilities, my job and my marriage. I had no choice but to see myself as I really was. I am nothing without him — dust — and I can do nothing without him. Now I understand that my life is not about me. It's about him. Knowing isn't enough. Even the devil knows about Jesus. It is knowing in my heart that Jesus died for me. My sins nailed him to the cross. And knowing I can have a relationship with this Savior makes all the difference in my life.

Scared to Death
The Story of Theresa Pattan
Written by Peggy Thompson

"You're not running a fever, Theresa. Do you have a sore throat?"

"No. I'm just so weak I have to lie down. May I call my mother to come get me?"

As she felt around my glands and throat with her fingers, a look of concern crossed her face.

"There's a knot right here at your throat. Did you know it was there?"

"Uh huh."

"Has your mom looked at it?"

"No. I haven't mentioned it to her."

"Why not?" she asked, looking a little alarmed.

Shrugging my shoulders, I said, "I don't know. It doesn't hurt or anything."

She got up and guided me to the cot in her office. "I think you should lie down while I call your mother."

The large-faced clock in the school nurse's office said 10:30 a.m. School had started at 8:00. Even before my mother dropped me off that morning, I knew I would never make it through the day.

About a month prior to this, I started having weak spells. My mom had taken me to the doctor, and he said it was some kind of virus and that she should keep me home from school for a few days.

I Will Not Go Quietly

Instead of getting better, I got worse, so she took me back to the doctor. He said I had a light case of mono and gave me some medication to take. That was two weeks ago, and now it was a real struggle for me to complete a day of school, let alone do my homework and chores at home.

She made the call, and I lay down on the cot and waited for my mother.

It was about 20 minutes later when Mom walked in the door and saw me lying there.

"Good morning, Mrs. Myers. I don't know what to think. This is the third day this week I have had to come get Theresa."

"I know she's on medication, and the doctor said it was okay for her to be in school, but I was wondering about something."

"What's that?"

"Have you noticed the lump on Theresa's neck, right near her throat area?"

"No!"

"Let me show you."

Mom and the school nurse both bent over me, and after Mrs. Myers showed my mother where she found the lump, my mom touched it gently. "What a curious thing. I can't imagine what it could be. A swollen gland?"

She turned her gaze to Mrs. Myers for some kind of affirmation.

"It doesn't seem to be located in a gland, but if I were you, I sure would take her back to the doctor and have it

SCARED TO DEATH

checked out."

"Absolutely."

She turned her gaze to meet mine, and I could see worry etched into fine lines on her face.

As she grabbed my coat from the hook on the wall, she said, "Let's go, honey. I want to get you home and to bed."

As I sat up, the room spun crazily and a wave of nausea gripped me.

"What's wrong, Theresa?"

"I feel sick."

My 11-year-old heart thumped hard in my chest. I was scared. My mother could see that, and she came and sat down beside me on the cot. Pulling me into her warm embrace, she kissed me softly on the side of my head and murmured, "Don't worry, baby. We're going to get you fixed up."

When we got home, Aunt Velma called out from the living room. "How's Theresa doing?"

"I'm going to put her to bed and then make an appointment with the doctor."

"Why don't you take her to a *real* doctor?"

My mom's face got red, and I could see her eyes flashing with anger, but she didn't say anything to my aunt.

Later, sitting at the dinner table, I couldn't eat, so I started making tracks in my mashed potatoes with the tines of my fork and stared as the gravy slowly filled them up like so many little rivers.

"Jim, we need to take Theresa to a specialist."

Dad didn't respond right away.

I Will Not Go Quietly

She lowered her gaze for a moment, then looked back up at him. In a soft voice she said, "What do you think, honey?"

With a big sigh, he looked at me for a moment and then back at Mom. "Yes, I think you should call Dr. Baker first thing in the morning and get a referral."

My dad reached over and took my small hand in his large one. "Mom made your favorite dinner tonight, honey. Try to eat. It'll make you feel better."

He gave me such a gentle, tender smile that I got up out of my chair and climbed into his lap. As I buried my head into the small space between his shoulder and his neck, he got up out of his chair and carried me into the living room where we sat together. He ran his fingers lightly through the soft brown silk of my hair — something I loved for him to do — and I tried to absorb some of the strength I could feel in his powerful body as the tears rolled down my cheeks.

They took me to a specialist in Bonners Ferry, Idaho, and ran some tests. Afterward, the three of us sat in the examining room and waited.

The door suddenly swooshed open, and a nurse came bustling into the room. "She can get dressed now. When you're ready, I'll meet you in the hall and show you to the doctor's office."

We were escorted into a large paneled office. The carpet was navy blue, and the pile was so thick it felt like my feet were sinking into patches of crushed velvet as I walked across the room to a chair. Navy blue drapes with a

Scared to Death

beige print framed each side of the large window behind his desk, and beige sheers hung in the middle. The paneling, the doctor's desk and all the furniture in the room were gleaming mahogany, and the touches of gold on his desk set, the lamp bases and other bric-a-brac around the room spoke volumes about a busy practice and a successful doctor.

It seemed we had been waiting for an eternity when the doctor finally walked briskly into the room. He was carrying a manila file folder. He greeted us with a nod and went immediately to his desk where he sat down.

As he checked over the lab reports, I noticed a frown gathering on his face. Raising his head, he focused his gaze on the faces of my parents. He did not beat around the bush. He was all business and efficiency.

"Theresa has lung cancer."

You could have heard a pin drop. Seconds went by, and there wasn't the slightest sound in the room. As he started scribbling on a piece of paper, he said, "I want you to take her to Spokane — tomorrow. I am giving you the name of a surgeon. He is one of the best in his field. The tumor needs to be removed, and Theresa will require follow-up treatment."

My mother started stammering. "But… but she's only 11…"

My father's face was anguished. He opened his mouth to speak but shut it again, remaining quiet. Tears gathered in his eyes.

I WILL NOT GO QUIETLY

"I know it's a shock for both of you, but it does happen."

Everything after that was a blur for me. I knew the word "cancer." To me it meant death. We had some relatives and friends who had died from various types of cancer.

Sitting in the chair, my breathing became ragged and my mouth felt dry, like it was full of cotton. *Am I going to die, God? But I'm not old! I'm just a kid!*

I was scared, confused, and the walls of the office seemed to pulsate with tension. Nothing felt real, and I didn't even notice that we had left the doctor's office until my dad was unlocking our car out in the parking lot.

My parents were scared and worried. I listened to their conversation, saw the looks on their faces.

The next day, we drove to Spokane and they admitted me to Sacred Heart Hospital. The following day, they did all my pre-surgery tests and that night, as I lay in bed, I found myself thinking about church and God. In Sunday school, they taught me about God. I had already accepted Christ, and although I believed he would take care of me, I was still scared. *Jesus, I know you have a home for me in heaven, but I don't want to go yet!* I was terrified to go to sleep, but after awhile, I fell into an exhausted and troubled slumber.

After the surgery and during my recovery, I was very lonely. We lived far away from the hospital, and my folks couldn't just drop everything and stay with me. My

SCARED TO DEATH

mother had three other kids to take care of, and my dad had to go to work. They came to see me every weekend.

When it was time for me to have radiation, my mother came and stayed with me for five weeks. We were both so surprised when I didn't lose my hair. There were a few thin spots, but I never lost it. We were elated.

Our joy over that small victory was short-lived, however. No sooner had they released me to go home than my mother was rushing me back again. I had become very ill. As I lay on the table in the examining room, I felt like I was drifting away, and at one point, I said, "Mom, will you take my hand? I want you to come with me."

She held my hand and stroked my brow while the doctor spoke to her. He lowered his voice, but somehow I was still able to hear him.

"We're going to fly her to Seattle for exploratory surgery. There may be more cancer somewhere in her body."

"She's very frail and sick. Can she withstand another surgery?" My mother was very apprehensive.

"Mrs. Lake, the odds are pretty slim that she will make it through the surgery, but she's so sick I'm not sure she will make it through the night."

"Don't touch her. Leave her alone. I want to call my husband."

My mother looked down at me. I wanted to go to sleep so badly, but she was saying something to me, so I fought the waves of darkness that were trying to claim me and struggled to hear her words that seemed to come from so far away.

I Will Not Go Quietly

"Theresa, I am going down the hall to the pay phone to call your dad. I will be right back, honey. Please just lie here quietly and rest."

My heavy eyelids shut for what seemed a moment, and when I opened them again, both my mom and dad were standing beside my bed. My eyes vaguely took in the unfamiliar surroundings.

"It's okay, honey. They moved you to a pretty little room."

"Theresa? It's me. Dad. I came to see how you were doing."

Headachy and groggy, I smiled and went back to sleep. The last thing I heard was, "We love you. You're going to be fine."

Much later, I found out that my dad made the one and a half hour drive from home to the hospital in record time. He also called my grandparents and our church. "We need prayer. Please get the prayer chain going."

Early the next morning, I was up and out of bed before the breakfast trays had been delivered. Both Mom and Dad were asleep in chairs against the wall. There was a playroom next door to my room and, being careful not to wake them, I went in there. I found a tricycle and started riding it all around the room. Because I had been so sick, I only weighed about 67 pounds, so I could still ride the little thing.

As I circled the room over and over again, I saw my parents standing in the doorway. They were watching me in wonder and amazement.

Scared to Death

The doctor came by on his early morning rounds and found us in there. He stood there speechless for some seconds. "I have absolutely no idea how this can be possible. We didn't expect her to make it through the night."

"It's a miracle. Anything is possible with God," my father told him.

It was necessary for me to have treatments throughout seventh and eighth grades. The Christian school I was attending let me do my schoolwork both at the hospital and at home. Just prior to my senior year, the doctors told my parents, "Everything is good," and they released me.

After I graduated from high school, my family and I moved from Montana to Oklahoma. Shoving God aside and forgetting all he had done for me, I was hungry for all kinds of experiences. Almost immediately, I fell in with a bad group and started drinking and partying. Trying to make up for lost time, within a few months, I met Glenn and fell madly in love.

After knowing each other for about eight months, we got married in May of 1986. Eight years later, after having two sons, we moved to Idaho where we continued to run around partying and drinking. We were rotten parents because we were too busy partying. When Glenn was drunk, he became verbally abusive, and once in a while, he would hit me. Reaching the point where I couldn't take it anymore, I divorced him. The boys and I were on our own for a while, and then I met Dale. In 1997, we married. We drank a little bit, too, but it wasn't long before I gave it up. The Lord was calling me back. I could feel the pull inside my heart, and five years after the wedding, I started going back to church. It was difficult at first because I was scared.

A good friend of mine and the mother of my youngest son's best friend, Maria Ward, "encouraged" me. We were both attending a school program and started horsing around outside. She tackled me and held me down until I agreed to go to church with her.

"How can I go back? Look at the things I've done!"

"Stop making excuses, Theresa. You know if you repent, God will forgive you."

A little voice inside me said, "It's time," but I honestly was afraid that I might get struck by lightning — or worse.

Three days later, I found myself going to Maria's church, Covenant House Christian Center. The following week, I went to a meeting in Spokane with her pastor's wife, Deloris, and some of the other ladies of the church. I didn't know any of these women, but they reached out to me with such love it was like they had known me all their lives. Their fellowship and support lifted me up. They became a very special, healing part of my life.

When my husband decided to attend church with me, I was ecstatic. He had never shown any interest in Jesus before, and I was thrilled that we were going to be able to share him — the one who was healing me, helping me and comforting me every day. I felt so blessed that now Dale was going to be a part of that, too.

About a year after he started going with me, he gave me a wonderful Mother's Day gift. One bright Sunday

SCARED TO DEATH

morning in May, we were hurrying to get ready for church. The boys were being difficult, and I was getting a little frustrated.

"I'm timing you! I expect both of you to be dressed and ready to go in 10 minutes!" I left them scurrying around and went into our bedroom. Dale followed me into the room.

"Theresa?"

Looking for my shoes, I was on my hands and knees poking around under the bed, somewhat distracted.

"Um hum?"

"I have a Mother's Day gift for you."

Sitting back on my heels, I turned my head toward my husband. He was standing there with a long, slender white box.

Tears filled my eyes as I stood up to accept his gift. "Oh, honey, I wasn't expecting you to get me anything. I know we're a little short this month."

"Open it."

Removing the lid, I brushed aside the white tissue paper. A single red rose, a beautiful bud, was nestled in the bottom of the box.

"There's a card," he said.

I felt around inside the box and found it. Opening the envelope, I read what he had written: "My darling wife, the red rose is a symbol of my love for you, but it also represents the mutual love of Christ and his church. Today in church, I am accepting Christ into my heart."

Gently putting the rose on the bed, I wrapped my arms

around his neck. "Dale, that's the most beautiful gift I have ever received."

My husband was now an active part of my new faith, and life seemed so good. But it didn't last very long. One Monday at work, I started feeling very weak, extremely fatigued and noticed I was retaining lots of water. Each day, the symptoms got progressively worse so that by Friday, I was pretty concerned.

"What's wrong? I can't do my job." As a nursing assistant, I had to be on my feet all the time.

That night during dinner, I talked to my husband about it. "This makes me nervous. When I was a little girl and had cancer, weakness was one of the very early symptoms."

"It makes me nervous, too. Sweetie, don't waste anymore time. Please! Go see the doctor."

My gaze rested briefly on my plate as I took a few sips of coffee. With a big sigh, I looked up.

"Yes, I know. I'll call the clinic Monday morning for an appointment."

"The sooner we know what's going on the better, Theresa."

By the end of the following week, I was in the doctor's office. After his examination and some tests, he said, "You have a heart valve that's messed up, Theresa. It needs to be fixed."

The information startled me. I hadn't even thought about my heart!

The doctor referred me to a specialist in Spokane. Officially now on leave of absence from my job, Dale and I drove up to see the specialist. "You need a bypass, and there's a valve that needs to be repaired."

After thinking about that for a minute or two, I looked at Dale and said, "Okay. I can handle that. I'll be back at work within a month."

They called me right after Christmas to let me know they had my surgery all set up for January 8th.

My husband, the two boys and I drove to Spokane on January 7th, the day before the surgery. We were also expecting my folks and our pastor to come up. All of us were nervous and on edge on the drive.

It was dark, around dinnertime, when we found ourselves in a town called Colfax.

"Hey, Mom, let's go to Arby's!" The boys loved to eat at Arby's.

"I'd rather have tacos."

"We passed a taco place a ways back," my husband said.

"No. There's no taco place in Colfax." I could hear the irritation in my voice.

"Theresa, I saw it with my own eyes." Now Dale sounded cranky.

"Well, you're wrong. There isn't a taco place within miles of here."

With a jerk of the wheel, he turned the car around. There was quite a bit of snow on the ground, and the car slid and swerved a little. We were both angry. Dale drove

I WILL NOT GO QUIETLY

back in the direction we had just come from, and within a couple of miles, there it was. Del Taco.

The men in my family wolfed their dinners down, but I just picked at mine. The argument had taken the edge off my appetite. As we left the restaurant, I turned to my husband and said, "Would you mind if I took a little walk right here in back of the restaurant? I think it would help my nerves, settle me down."

"Sure. Let's all go."

Touching his sleeve lightly, my gaze fastened onto his. He read me correctly. I needed a few minutes to be alone, to walk off some tension. I didn't want to admit it, but I was scared.

"Okay. We'll wait in the car for you. Don't wander too far, and don't be too long, okay? It's starting to snow again."

Zipping up my parka, I pulled on a knitted snow hat and some nice warm mittens. Stepping off the asphalt parking lot onto the snow-covered ground, I was thankful that I had worn my snow boots. There were several inches of snow on the ground.

The lights from the restaurant shone on the snow, and it glistened and sparkled as I began to walk. Spotting a pretty little area not too far away, I headed toward a small grove of birch, bare of leaves, with a scattering of dark spruce nearby. As I walked, I thought about life in general, all the change and uncertainty. My family and I were now transitioning from a familiar past to an uncertain future.

Scared to Death

Finally out of the light and enveloped by darkness, I walked up a little rise and stopped to catch my breath. Standing there, hands in my pockets, everything was white: the trees, the sky, the ground, the very air around me. I stood absolutely still for a few moments and swayed a little bit in the gusts of wind that had begun to blow.

Shivering with the cold, I turned back and started walking to the car. I couldn't help thinking that we humans are always traveling, but often we don't know where we are going. Our safekeeping lies in God himself.

Returning to the car, I got in and shut the door. There was no way I could know that my memory, my total recall, was snapping shut at the same time.

Dale told me that the morning of January 8th, he drove me to the hospital. He said Pastor Bear, our pastor from our church in Idaho, drove three hours to Sacred Heart Hospital and entered my room just before the surgery. We talked for a while, and then he prayed for me. As nurses wheeled my rickety gurney into the hallway, Pastor Bear took my hand, gazed deeply into my eyes and said, "You're going to be okay."

As mask-clad nurses wheeled me down the sterile hospital halls to the operating room, I couldn't help wondering what he knew that I didn't.

A doctor inserted a needle into my arm, and blackness fell over me like a huge, dark blanket. They had just put me under the anesthesia.

Dr. Coffman was going to do this surgery alone, but when he made the incision, he discovered things were worse than he had expected. There was a hole in my heart, two valves needed to be replaced, another valve needed to be repaired, and I needed a bypass. Very surprised and not expecting such extensive damage, he had to call in another surgeon.

They hooked me up to the heart-lung machine, and the two surgeons and their assistants began the delicate and complicated process of repairing my heart. At one point, Dr. Coffman gently lifted a piece of the aorta and shook his head in disbelief.

"Theresa is very petite. We need smaller body parts for her."

In order to get a "fit," a call was placed immediately to a children's hospital in town. As Dr. Coffman stopped and waited in the middle of this surgery, he was filled with the anxiety of valuable time being lost as they waited for the parts they needed to be flown in by helicopter. The surgery, which was supposed to have taken about four hours, quickly turned into a 14-hour process.

In the waiting room, my parents, my husband, our two boys, Pastor Bear and two of my friends from Covenant House sat waiting nervously, glancing at the clock about every five minutes.

"What's taking so long? It's been five hours," Pastor Bear began thinking to himself. "This seems quite long for a heart surgery."

Six hours passed, then seven, and Pastor Bear really became concerned. As my relatives and friends began pacing back and forth, worry etched on their faces, he cried out to God. "God, you told me she would be okay!"

Holding onto that faith, that promise, was the only thing that kept him going. It enabled him to help calm my family. As more time went by, he began to pray earnestly for me, and he continued to pray until the surgery was over.

About 10 hours into the surgery, I suffered a massive stroke.

One of the doctors came into the waiting room where my family and friends were frantic with worry. His surgical mask still covered his nose and mouth, but his eyes betrayed a weary, almost defeated look. As his gaze scanned the room, he saw my husband and, confidence sagging, walked over to him to talk. He was apologetic and frazzled when he spoke.

He reached up and untied his mask. It fell loosely around his neck.

"Your wife has suffered a stroke. We'll complete the surgery, but we just don't have much hope for her."

As he saw the stunned, shocked look in my husband's gaze and the tears starting to fill his eyes, he reached out and put his hand on Dale's shoulder. "I'm so sorry."

My parents gripped one another tightly. Pastor Bear was on the phone immediately calling home.

"You guys need to start praying. We need lots of prayer — now!"

People all over the country prayed for me, some as far away as Pennsylvania.

I Will Not Go Quietly

The surgery was completed after 14 hours. My heart had been mended, but I was unconscious, and the stroke had caused damage to my entire body.

My husband told me I was in a coma for 13 days. My entire left side was paralyzed. He would stay with me one week, and then my mother would switch with him the following week. They took turns like this so that the kids wouldn't miss school.

They hooked me up to every kind of machine you can imagine, including a breathing machine. There were so many tubes, Dale was afraid they might make a mistake trying to figure out which one to use.

The boys were 14 and 11, and they were so scared. Dale brought the youngest to visit me.

"It's going to look a little scary, okay? You're not used to seeing this kind of stuff, and Mom is very sick."

"Yeah. Okay, Dad."

The minute they came into the room, Brandon started crying.

"Oh, no! Mom! Mom!" He couldn't handle it, and he turned around and walked out sobbing.

The oldest, Chris, did great. He held my hand, talked to me, even prayed. He tried to get me to wake up.

My mother and my husband were pretty uptight about the breathing machine. Whenever the medical staff tried to remove the tube, I would stop breathing and they had to put it back. They did this so many times that they damaged my left vocal cord. That did it for my husband. Dale told them to leave the breathing tube alone. "Just leave it in!"

Dale was driving home one night. He was more than halfway there when he got a call on his cell phone. "What do you guys want?"

"We took the breathing tube out, and she quit breathing, so we're going to have to put it back in."

"You were told not to do that! And besides that, her father and mother are over at the hotel. You need to call them!"

Dale called my parents himself and told them what was going on. They were so upset they found the chaplain of the hospital and put him on the phone with my husband. In his frustration and anger, Dale really tore into the poor man. He was blowing off steam because they weren't supposed to touch me unless they asked first. My parents read them the riot act.

My mother and father were very protective of me and a little rough on the people that came to see me. They didn't care whether they were from the church or not. They didn't understand the faith or my relationship with the church and my fellow Christians, but were making sure that things that weren't supposed to happen didn't happen. They loved me so much, and they wanted only the best for me.

While I was paralyzed, everyone tried to get me to move. They wanted me to move my left side, but I only moved the right. My mom was in the room and they told her, "We have got to get her to come out of this."

I Will Not Go Quietly

"Watch this," Mom replied, as she remembered something about the tenacity of my spirit.

"Theresa! You can't move your arms, you can't move your legs, and you will never walk again. You will be paralyzed for the rest of your life, and you will be in a wheelchair."

All of a sudden, I raised my left arm up, wiggled my hand and fingers, and then I put it down again.

The nurse was floored. "How did you get her to do that?"

"You tell that girl she can't do something, and she will do it just to prove you wrong!"

One day, the doctor took my husband and my dad aside. "We think there's about a 0 percent possibility that she's going to make it. You guys need to seriously think about taking all the tubes out and letting her go."

"No, leave her alone!" My husband believed in me. He knew how determined and positive I was about things, and he trusted God to revive me. He believed God would bring me back just like he had promised Pastor Bear.

The next morning, I woke up. Everyone was dumbfounded. They were sure they had witnessed a miracle.

The nurse went running for a doctor. When he came into the room, he started asking me questions.

"Theresa, where are you?"

"I'm in Colfax, in the basement of a hospital."

"Why are you saying that?"

"Dale left me in Colfax because we fought over tacos."

In my subconscious, I thought my husband was mad at

SCARED TO DEATH

me.

They kept me in ICU for another week, and then they moved me up to the heart floor. I had been in ICU for three weeks. The only thing I remember about the day they moved me out of ICU is how badly I had to go to the bathroom, and the catheter had been removed.

As my folks sat by my bed, I said in a weak voice, "Mom, I have to go potty really bad."

Too late, my mother saw I had wet the bed, and she went looking for a nurse. While my bedding was being changed, I asked her, "Am I still in the recovery room?"

When she told me I had been in a coma, and for how long, I was stunned because I thought I had just come out of surgery.

They sat there and told me the whole story. It was a very creepy feeling to find out that I had lost a month of my life.

Dale asked the doctors why so many things had gone wrong with my heart.

"We can't say with 100 percent certainty, but we think the radiation treatments she received as a young girl were the cause of the problem. They were on her left side, and there's no family history of any of these heart problems."

One morning, two physical therapists came into my room. They were young guys and very nice. "We need to see how much therapy you are going to need on that left side."

"Why?"

"Because you are paralyzed."

I Will Not Go Quietly

"I am? Okay. Whatever you say."

They brought a wheelchair into the room and pushed it up close to my bed. "We want you to hold onto the back of the chair for support and try to walk."

Turning back the covers on my bed, I got up and slowly walked out the door. When I got too weak and tired, they put me in the wheelchair to take me back to my room. The paralysis had affected my diaphragm on the left side and my left lung. As they were pushing me back to my room, the doctor showed up. "What's this?"

"She walked the first half of this trip. We're on our way back!"

A mistake was made one night at dinnertime. My dinner tray was sumptuous looking — roast beef, carrots, mashed potatoes — I thought I had gone to heaven.

With a good grip on the tray, I went for the roast beef. In no time at all, I had taken a couple of quick bites and started choking and gagging.

Dale reached for the tray. "Theresa, you're not supposed to eat that."

"You touch this tray, and you're going to have to fight me for it!"

"I'm going to get you another tray."

"No, you're not!"

He went out of the room and told the nurse about the mistake. "She's supposed to be on a soft diet."

Within moments, they brought me another tray with the food I was supposed to be eating. "I don't want this baby food. I want the other stuff, the real food." I still had

Scared to Death

a feeding tube in me and a drain in my lung, but I sure wanted that roast beef.

As I neared the end of a week on the heart floor, the doctor said he wanted to operate to see if my damaged vocal cord could be fixed. The day before I was supposed to be discharged, they put some collagen right up against it, and it wasn't long before I got my voice back.

Lovingly, and with relief, my husband teased as he told visitors, "Dang! They could have waited a little bit longer. I was enjoying the peace and quiet!"

My husband and I had gone to hell and back together, and it was a frightening road. We are closer because of it, and our marriage has improved.

Through it all, I grew a lot, spiritually. I am closer to God than ever before, and I *know* he answers prayer. My husband is a lot closer to God, too. He is usually the first person to tell someone about the miracle of prayer.

There are residual problems that I'm learning to live with. My memory isn't that great, and my left lung isn't working like it should. I get tired if I walk very much. My pulmonary doctor said I'll need a lung transplant by the time I'm 50.

"No! No more of that stuff for me. God will take care of it."

My pastor tried to encourage everyone as things started going downhill fast. He cried out to God, "You told me she was going to be all right, and that's what I told her. Lord, she has to be all right. I believe you. I *must* believe you." He got a month of sermons out of that. They were

I WILL NOT GO QUIETLY

called "I Must Believe!" When God tells you something, you must believe it.

This is the first time I have talked about all of this, the whole thing from beginning to end. I knew it would be difficult to talk about it, and I almost didn't do it. But I believe God wanted me to do it, and if it helps even one person, if only one soul is saved, then it was worth it. I thank God for the love of Jesus Christ and his mercy in my life.

Those who live in the shelter of the Most High will find rest in the shadow of the Almighty. This I declare of the Lord: He alone is my refuge, my place of safety; he is my God, and I am trusting him. For he will rescue you from every trap and protect you from the fatal plague. He will shield you with his wings. He will shelter you with his feathers. His faithful promises are your armor and protection. Do not be afraid of the terrors of the night, nor fear the dangers of the day, nor dread the plague that stalks in darkness, nor the disaster that strikes at midday. Though a thousand fall at your side, though ten thousand are dying around you, these evils will not touch you. (Psalm 91:1-7)

THE BLACK SHEEP
THE STORY OF TRISTAN HARVEY
WRITTEN BY PEGGY THOMPSON

"Come on in, Tristan."

"No! The water's too cold." Sitting on a rock in my new swim trunks, I watched the river as it slowly flowed by, gurgling and bubbling.

"But it's not. Honest!"

Tentatively, I dipped the toes of my left foot into the water. It was warm, like bath water. "It's warm!"

"Told ya!" my brother yelled back.

Easing myself off the rock into the rippling water, I felt its warmth encircle my body up to the waist. Relaxing, I just let go and enjoyed the feeling.

Reluctantly, I started to wake. Fighting the feeling, I didn't want to come out of my warm cocoon of sleep. My eyelids sensed the light coming through the window, and I squeezed my eyes tightly shut, trying to make it go away. Clinging to a wisp of my dream, it evaporated like fog, and I yielded myself to the inevitable fact of waking up.

There was a loud knock on my bedroom door.

"Time to get up. Breakfast is ready."

A sickening feeling started churning in my stomach as I became aware of what I had done. The familiar wetness spread all the way up the back of my pajama pants to the waistband. Hot tears stung the backs of my eyes and feelings of humiliation and frustration washed over me.

I Will Not Go Quietly

My bedroom door opened, and my mother came in.

"Didn't you hear me call you? You're going to be late for school if you don't get a move on."

She quickly walked to my closet, took a clean shirt off a hanger and grabbed my jeans from a clothes peg on the back of the closet door.

With both hands covering my eyes, I lay there silently crying.

She walked over to my bed. "#@!#@! Not again!"

The disappointment and disgust in her voice penetrated to my soul, and I wanted to curl up and die. So many times, I had heard her say how tired she was of having to constantly wash my bedding.

Pulling the covers back, she snapped, "Get to the bathroom! You know what to do!"

In a fit of temper, she started taking the wet sheets and blankets off the bed.

My brother, Richard, poked his head inside the doorway to my room. "Hey, Mom. Did Tristan wet the bed again?"

"Never mind, Richard. Go eat your breakfast."

There were four kids in our family. My oldest brother and my sister were grown and had left home. At age 10, I was the youngest. Richard was the closest in age to me, four years older, and he was the favorite. I lived in his shadow.

After quickly cleaning myself up, I got dressed and hurried to breakfast.

The others were eating when I silently slipped into my

THE BLACK SHEEP

chair. As I tentatively took a bite of toast, my mother's voice boomed, "Tristan, how old are you?"

Without lifting my gaze, I said, "10." There was a lump in my throat, and it was almost impossible to swallow my toast.

"10. 10 years old and still wetting the bed."

My brother snickered.

Sitting there, head in my hands, I wasn't able to eat anything.

"We may have to housebreak you. Just like the dog," she continued.

Richard spoke out loudly. "Yeah! We rubbed his nose in his own mess!"

"Right," my mother responded, giving Richard a fond look.

The thought horrified me. *Would she really rub my nose in it?*

Except for my father, all eyes were on me. He never interfered when my mother scolded us. He was a quiet, mild-mannered man, very unassuming.

I was miserable and just wanted to get out of there.

"That was a wonderful book report you wrote for school, Richard," my mother's soft voice said.

As I glanced in her direction, I noticed that she was already underway with her daily drinking. The color of the liquid in her glass, along with the foam on top, was very familiar to me. Beer. By the time I got home from school, she would be falling down drunk.

"Don't you have to give an oral report today, too?"

I Will Not Go Quietly

Striving for my own recognition, I broke into the conversation. "Mom, did you see my report card?"

"Sorry to say I did. As usual, it wasn't very good. Now shut up!"

Ever since I could remember, I was starved for recognition. No one in the family ever praised me for anything. They didn't think I would ever amount to much. It was always Richard that they talked about. He couldn't do anything wrong, never got in trouble. And Richard never wet the bed.

It was painfully obvious that my family, including grandparents, aunts and uncles, thought Richard was something special, whereas they didn't think much of me at all. It got to the point where I thought, "That's just the way it is," and I decided to live up to their expectations.

When it was time for the school bus, I grabbed my books and sweater. On the way out the front door, I watched as my mom took another gulp of beer. Worry consumed me because I was so afraid she would seriously hurt herself sometime when she was drunk.

"See you later," she called and waved to us from the front door.

When we got home later that afternoon, Richard took off. He had his own plans, but I always went seeking my mother to reassure myself she was okay.

Walking into the kitchen, I grabbed an apple out of the green fruit bowl on the table as I went by. Mom was at the sink.

"Mom?"

THE BLACK SHEEP

She turned away from the sink and walked right by me as if I hadn't spoken. She lurched, and her gait was unsteady. There was no sign of recognition in her bleary eyes. Her face looked sort of rubbery, all her features seemed to droop.

Weaving her way to the utility room, I saw she was headed directly for an empty apple crate Dad had left on the floor in there the night before.

"Look out, Mom!" But it was too late. She stumbled over the crate and fell to the floor.

"Mom! Mom!" Racing over to where she had fallen, it took all of my strength to help her up. Her cheek was already beginning to bruise.

"S'al right. Lemme alone."

Like a zombie she weaved her way back through the kitchen, down the hall and into the bathroom with me right on her heels. Once inside she stood at the sink for a moment, then sank like a sack of potatoes to the floor. She had passed out, and I wasn't going to be able to move her.

Not knowing what to do, and because I was frightened, I went into the living room where I sank down into a large armchair to wait for my father. He didn't always come right home from work, and I anxiously picked at the knobby fabric of the chair, hoping with all my heart that today would be an exception.

When I heard his car in the driveway, I was terribly relieved, and I walked to the door, opened it and stood there, waiting for him.

"Mom's in the bathroom."

I WILL NOT GO QUIETLY

He gave me a funny look, like "So what?"

"She fainted or something."

He made his way to the bathroom, and I watched as he took a cold, wet cloth and wiped Mom's face, patted her hands, and finally, picked her up and carried her to the bedroom where he laid her on the bed to sleep it off.

I was 12 when I finally stopped wetting my bed.

My father didn't drink. His thing was gambling. When I was growing up there were gambling halls, special rooms at the back of stores, where the guys would get together and play cards. My dad was such a good gambler he almost always won. He supplemented our income with his winnings, but he and my mom had some nasty fights about that — and her drinking.

Often when I got home from school in the afternoon, Mom would collar me.

"Come on, son. We're gonna find that no good father of yours and haul his #@! home."

Drunk as she was, she would make me walk for miles and miles with her. We checked all the gambling halls until we found him — then she sent me in to get him out.

"Dad?" Pushing my way through the smoke-filled room, I finally saw him, head bent over, studying his hand of cards. When I got to his chair, he lifted his gaze and gave me a sheepish grin. The other guys at the table teased him unmercifully which embarrassed him and made me uncomfortable, too.

"Mom's waiting outside."

"Go back out there and tell her I'll be there soon."

The Black Sheep

"You tell him to hurry up!" She turned me around by the shoulders and physically pushed me back toward the shop.

My dad's way of getting back at my mom was to take his time, drag things out, not hurry himself in any way. This made me panicky because she was waiting outside, drunk and angry, expecting me to get him out of there. They were both using me to get back at each other.

In eighth grade, my teacher, Mr. Demco, loved to give me a bad time. He even put me down as no good. He never called me by my first name. He always used my last name.

"Hey, Harvey! What are you going to be when you grow up?"

When I didn't answer, he yelled at me.

"Come up here! I'm talking to you!"

Shuffling up front, head down, hands in my pockets, he made me stand there in front of the whole class while he put me down.

One time, I shocked him and myself and stood up to him.

"You're going to be a bum, right? You're going to dig ditches."

"No, I'm going to fill them up!"

"Aw, go sit down."

As I returned to my seat, I heard him mumble under his breath, "Bum will never amount to anything."

When I was 14, my dad went to work for a home improvement company as an expediter. I hung around with

I Will Not Go Quietly

the construction crews and decided I wanted to have my own construction company someday.

At the dinner table one night, I got all excited about it and started telling my folks about it.

"Mom, when I'm old enough, I'm going to have my own construction company!"

"Yeah, right." She gave me a look that said, "What a joke."

"No, I mean it!"

"If you got grades like your brother, Richard, if you were as good as him, I believe you could do that," Mom added. "Richard will be able to do whatever he wants. Tristan, I'm afraid you'll be lucky if you can do something where you can earn a living."

Slam! Put down and trod on again. How it screamed in my soul — you'll never be good enough.

When I was 16, I needed a job and decided to approach the man who owned a local gas station.

After I cleaned myself up, I hoped I looked decent. Then I went to the gas station. When there was a lull in the activity, I approached him. He was a big man, very overweight, and he looked strong.

"Hi, my name is Tristan. I'm looking for a job."

He was sitting behind a desk that was cluttered with tools, greasy rags and an out-of-date calendar with pictures of old cars on it. Leaning back in his chair, it creaked and groaned with the weight of his body. He looked at me for a long moment.

"What can you do?"

THE BLACK SHEEP

"Uh, well, I can do construction work. I'm real good with tools, all kinds. And I work on cars all the time with my friends."

"What did you say your name was?"

"Tristan. Tristan Harvey."

"Tr... Tr... #@#, I can't pronounce that!"

He stood up and stuck his hand out to shake mine. "I'm going to call you Trusty. Okay with you?"

My heart leaped in my breast. He was going to hire me! "Sure. That's fine."

As we shook hands, he said, "My name is Harold."

He hired me on the spot, and I worked for $1.00 an hour, $40 a week.

Harold was a womanizer and a drunk. Many times, he didn't show up for work because he knew I could handle it. "Trusty, be sure you live up to your name now."

Some of my friends also worked for Harold. He would fix them up with questionable females. Being a 16-year-old kid, I wanted him to fix me up, too. He always told me he was going to do it, but he never did.

"Oh, you always say you're going to fix me up, but you never do."

He gave me a long look. "Trusty, I'm not going to do it. You're different. You're not like these other kids. Some-day you're going to be something."

He thought highly of me; he thought I was special. A rush of pride surged through me. Harold was the first person in my life to give me recognition and a feeling of self-worth. I hung onto that for dear life.

I Will Not Go Quietly

In my neighborhood, there was a nightclub for teens. The only difference between ours and the adult ones was that we weren't served booze. In the backroom, there was usually a pool table. One night, I was playing pool by myself, practicing, and the leader of this gang walked in with about 10 of his guys. I knew all of them from high school.

"Hey, you know, you're playing pool on my pool table."

"No, I don't think so. I don't see your name on it. I'm playing pool here."

He punched me in the mouth and expected me to punch him back. All his guys began moving in on me, surrounding me, and I knew I was going to get stomped. At that very moment, a police officer came through the door, scanned the room to check it out and, as he was leaving, I pushed my way through the guys and followed him. I went and sat down in the main part of the club, ordered a glass of pop and watched the band perform. After a couple of minutes, assuming I had said something to the officer, the gang leader came and sat down at my table across from me.

"Hey, what did you tell that cop?"

"I didn't tell that cop anything. I don't need his help with you. I can't fight 10 of you, but I'll take you on anytime you want!"

"You know what? I always thought you were a punk and that you weren't cool, but you know…"

He invited me to be a part of his gang. It didn't matter to me that it was a gang, he just validated me. He said I

THE BLACK SHEEP

was cool; I was good enough. I was accepted.

Soon after I went to work for Harold, my mother and I had a major blowout. When I came home one evening, she and my dad were fighting and arguing.

"You're just as bad as…" She was riding my dad pretty hard.

"Shut up! What makes you think you're so special?"

"We need to get a divorce!"

"You've been saying that for years. Why don't you go ahead?"

"You're a problem…" She turned her head and saw me in the kitchen for the first time, even though I had been standing there listening and watching.

They stopped arguing and watched as I walked to the refrigerator, took out a bottle of beer and stood there with it in my hand.

"*Here's* the problem!"

Enraged, I threw the bottle on the floor. Broken glass and beer flew everywhere.

"I'm outta here!" I yelled.

I moved out, and I quit school.

My mother's "other side" was incredible. When she wasn't drinking, she was one of the kindest, most compassionate people you could ever know. She was even the local Cub Scout leader.

My father was the softball coach for our local church. Although my parents only went once or twice a year, they made sure I went to Sunday school where I got a "storybook" version of religion. They taught me Biblical stories, but I never heard anything about being "saved" or "born again."

One day in Sunday school, the teacher asked, "If somebody was going to kill you but said they wouldn't if you denied that God or Jesus existed, what would you do?"

That put a hunger in my heart to know if God was real. As I grew up, that question would come to my mind every once in a while.

In order to complete my high school education, I went to Toledo University in Toledo, Ohio, and earned my GED. After that, I periodically attended a vocational college.

When I was 21, I had broken free from gang activity, and I created my first construction company. Because of my very low self-esteem and the way I had been put down all my life, I felt like a success with my business. Work was not a problem for me.

My relationships with women were a different story.

Because of my low self-esteem, I was very timid about relationships of any kind. This made me easy prey when it came to women. I was so starved for recognition, looking so desperately for acceptance, that although I wasn't an initiator, I immediately accepted any woman that "came on" to me. These lustful relationships were a way I could "validate myself."

At age 18, I got a girl pregnant and we got married. We had a son and a dysfunctional marriage. We were unfaithful to each other.

"I don't want to be married. I want a boyfriend.

THE BLACK SHEEP

Heaven knows you sure have plenty of girlfriends."

"Fine! I'm tired of being chained to you anyway."

We decided to split up after two and a half years of marriage. Shortly after we split up, she discovered she was pregnant again, and she delivered our second son about a week before our divorce was final.

My ex-wife made some very bad choices in her lifestyle and the type of men she kept in her life. Eventually, I applied for custody of our sons and when I finally got the boys, I was already into my second marriage.

My second wife and I had two children of our own, a boy and a girl. We encountered some severe problems trying to become "one big, happy family."

"I don't want those boys around! They will ruin *my* kids!"

"What do you want me to do? Get rid of them?"

"No. I want a divorce!"

A divorce was the last thing in the world that I wanted, and I was heartbroken.

"Dana, I love you very much. Please don't divorce me. We can work this out."

She wouldn't listen to me.

My new companion was drugs. All of my friends were into heroin, pot, speed and opium out of the water pipe, so I joined them. Then I started to drink. As much as I despised alcohol and what it had done to my parents, I decided it was okay to go share a beer with the guys. The real reason was the same old reason: fear of rejection.

Driving down the highway one day, I spotted a very

I Will Not Go Quietly

attractive gal hitchhiking. Slowing the car, I pulled up alongside the shoulder of the road beside her. The window was down on the passenger side, and she leaned on the frame and a little bit into the car.

"Are you okay?" I asked. "This stretch of road is a little isolated."

"Are you going into town? I need a ride into town."

She was petite, about 5'3", with a wonderful figure. One of my hands could span the width of her waist. She had short, curly red hair, sparkling blue eyes and a peaches-and-cream complexion. She wore battered but clean jeans, a tee shirt in a flattering shade of green, and thong sandals. She carried a sweater and a shopping bag full to the brim with what appeared to be more clothes. She was young. Very young.

"How old are you?"

"Old enough."

"A smart talker, huh?"

She lowered her gaze, her thick, dark lashes brushing the rise of flesh on the uppermost part of her cheekbone. "I'm sorry. I didn't mean to be rude."

"Get in." There was no way I was going to leave her all alone on a deserted stretch of road.

We were driving on a winding two-lane road, gradually climbing to a mesa that afforded a sweeping view below. The hillsides were covered with pines, and their scent was carried on the soft breeze that was blowing through the car. It was difficult to imagine such beautiful landscape just 10 miles outside of town.

THE BLACK SHEEP

After a few minutes, and determined to break the silence between us, I asked, "Do you know anyone in town?"

"My aunt lives there. I'm going to stay with her for a while."

I turned my head and gave her a quick glance. She was looking at me, and when our gazes met, she gave me a quick, small smile. "I'm pregnant."

That was the last thing in the world I expected to hear her say. Before I could think of something to say, her story poured out.

"My boyfriend left me the minute I told him about the baby. He wouldn't drive me to my aunt's place, so I've been thumbing it for two days."

"What have you done at night? It gets cold out here."

She cleared her throat. "I've been lucky to get rides from guys."

The unstated obvious hung in the air.

"I've had sex with hundreds of men. Sometimes they give me a couple of joints or some coke."

"What's your name?"

"Laura. I'm 18, well, a month shy."

"I was thinking about stopping at McDonald's for something to eat when I pull into town. You hungry?"

She didn't answer, so I turned my head just enough to be able to see her face. She was still looking at me, but tears were running down her satin-smooth cheeks. In that moment, I decided not only to feed her at McDonald's, but to take care of her somehow.

I Will Not Go Quietly

"There's tissues in the glove box."

We rode the rest of the way in silence. Pulling into town and then into McDonald's, I ordered two Big Mac's, two large orders of fries and two Pepsis. I found a little tree-lined side street, and we parked and indulged in some dashboard dining and more conversation. It was no surprise to me when Laura confided that she didn't have an aunt living in town.

We went to my apartment. I felt so sorry for her. She looked like a waif, and she was pretty beaten up by the world. As it turned out, her parents lived near Lake Erie. Without a blink of an eye, I made a huge decision.

"Laura, we're going to call your parents and let them know you're all right. Then we're going to tell them I am the villain that got you pregnant and we want to get married. You will need their consent since you're not 18 yet, so we'll have to drive up there and get them to sign for you. After that, we're going to get married and move to Florida." Whenever I saw people suffer the abuse of rejection, I wanted to help, not realizing my own dysfunction — that I was probably as bad off as they were. In reality, I just made things worse.

It was wild. It was bizarre. But moving to Florida had been on my mind anyway. A friend of mine had been bugging me to come down there. Construction work had really dried up in Ohio.

"Hey, come on down here, Tristan. We've got this job we are waiting on. In the meantime, we can sell vacuum cleaners."

THE BLACK SHEEP

One of the ways I had made money when I was around 17 was selling vacuum cleaners for major companies, so I had experience doing that.

Laura and I went, and we had barely arrived when I realized, "Man, I did something stupid here. I had no business marrying this girl. How ignorant can I be?" I was 27 years old and pretty disgusted with myself.

Making up my mind to send Laura back to her parents, it wasn't long before I allowed myself to be drawn into a relationship with another woman — again.

It was a warm, sunny day when I set out to sell vacuum cleaners. My first stop was a well kept but small yellow and white house, and when I knocked on the door, an elderly lady well into her 80s opened it. She was the sweetest looking old woman I had ever seen. Her hair was white and soft looking, like cotton, and her blue eyes twinkled through little glasses perched on the end of her nose. She was short and plump and wore a black and white polka dot dress. She wore lace-up shoes and rolled down nylons that stopped just below the knee.

"Hi. My name is Tristan Harvey, and I'm selling Kirby vacuum cleaners. I'd love to do a demonstration for you." She needed a new vacuum like she needed a hole in the head.

"My name is Mrs. Grimm." Her voice was a little high pitched and soft. "Please come in. I'd love to see what that machine can do."

After the demonstration, we were sitting there talking. She told me she was a retired minister and started telling me about the Lord. My heart was so hungry I sat there listening, hanging on every word. Mrs. Grimm referred to some of the Biblical stories I had learned as a kid. It felt like a soft whisper gently floated through the air past my head. "You can find acceptance with the Lord."

She made us some tea and talked about Jesus, and I was really enjoying it.

Mrs. Grimm decided to buy the vacuum cleaner. As I left her house, I felt like I was on the verge of something wonderful in my life, and I could hardly contain my excitement.

The next day, I was told the finance company had turned her down for credit. It was $400.

"They're too old, Tristan. They won't live long enough to pay the contract. Look, they listed their credit cards in the financial information section of the contract. You go back and tell them it would be better if they put this on their credit card."

It was a Saturday when I went back to Mrs. Grimm's house with the story. It was eating at me because it was untrue. It was better for us, not her. We segued off onto the subject of Jesus again, and she told me she went to a Pentecostal church. She also explained the baptism of the Holy Spirit. She told me about a *real* experience she had. As I listened to her, something inside me was saying, "That's what I'm looking for. I need something real. No storybook stuff." It started to register with me that Jesus was real.

There I was, 27 years old, a 200-pound weightlifter,

and this tiny, frail woman had me in the palm of her hand. She reached over and patted me on the knee. "Honey, if you would give your heart to the Lord Jesus, he would do so much for you."

By this time, I was getting uncomfortable because I knew I was going to have to make a decision about a commitment.

"Well, you know, that's just why I don't."

"What do you mean?"

"I would feel like I was using him."

She took my heart in her hands as she looked at me and said, "Honey, you can't use God. He knows everything. He'll use you."

My heart melted. She was speaking to me as if I were a little child. This was the second time in my entire life I had been affirmed in the right way. The first was Harold. When she said God would use me that seemed so absurd because I knew I was no good. That's all I had heard all my life, and I believed it.

"Do you want to pray to ask the Lord into your heart?"

"Yes, I do."

At that moment, I sensed the presence of the Lord and the presence of evil in that place. It seemed the Lord was saying, "I love you. I want you. You are my child."

The devil was snarling, "This is stupid! Get out of here! This is a joke!"

"Get out of here, and leave him alone." There was a strong sense of the evil presence leaving and the Lord coming into my life. I have felt him every day of my life

I WILL NOT GO QUIETLY

since.

Mrs. Grimm had told me about her Pentecostal church, so I decided to find one and start going. I told them I had given my heart to the Lord, and they were so gracious to me. They never said I was a dirty sinner. They just shared God's truth with me, and we talked about how I needed to change my life to follow God.

One guy had a ministry, praying for people to help them get free from spiritual bondages or influences. I attended one of his sessions. He and I started talking together, and we ended up talking for hours. Afterward, I agreed to let him pray for me.

When he finished praying, he told me, "I believe God has set you free from lust and all this stuff." But I knew nothing had happened.

It was a hot Florida night, about 2 a.m., and we started walking down the sidewalk in back of the church. As we were saying goodbye, I said, "I think the Lord understands that I want to send this girl back to her parents, and I think he understands where I am in this relationship."

"Bro, I love you, but I wouldn't want to be in your shoes."

At that very moment, I literally felt like a two-edged sword cut through me from my left shoulder to my right hip. It was hot, sharp and real. I had never heard any scripture or anyone talk about this, but from that moment on, I was somehow set free. I never had to deal with those feelings again. It was revealed to me that there could be genuine love in relationships. I had never known.

THE BLACK SHEEP

It would be some time later in my life that I would hear the Bible described as a "two-edged sword, cutting asunder to the bone and the marrow."

Immediately, I went home and apologized to my wife and reconciled our marriage. Then I gave up my girlfriend. "I can't do this anymore."

Within six months of finding a church in Tampa, the congregation asked me to help out with some things. After a year, I became a youth pastor.

A thought took hold of me, and my heart told me if I ever was going to do anything right, this was it. Two years after I got saved, I went back to see Mrs. Grimm.

One Saturday morning, I knocked on her door. When she opened it, I said, "Hi there, Mrs. Grimm. Do you remember me?"

After looking me up and down, her sweet, thin voice said, "No."

"I'm the fella you bought the vacuum cleaner from a few years ago."

"Oh, honey! Come on in!"

She sat in an armchair, and I sat on the ottoman right in front of her. "Are you still serving the Lord? What are you doing?"

"I just had to come by and see you. I'm in ministry, and I'm a youth pastor."

"Oh, that's so wonderful! I can't wait to get to church tomorrow."

"Why?"

"Because everybody in my church told me that you

pretended to be saved just so I would buy that vacuum cleaner."

One of the biggest treasures of my life was the joy I was able to give back to Mrs. Grimm. She brought me to the Lord and helped change my life so that I could help others.

Within five years, Laura and I had moved back to our hometown, close to her parents. My construction work was always out of town. Although I don't know why they did it, her parents convinced her that I wasn't really working, that I was messing around, so she decided to leave me. When she left, she immediately went back to her old lifestyle. That was it for me. I was never going to get married again.

My two boys and I went back to Tennessee where I knew some ministers, and they asked me to help them with their tent ministries. The boys and I moved into a small place of our own, and I became the lead guy for the tent ministries during the summer. Then we moved to the headquarters of one of the ministries in Tennessee, and I went to work in a Christian school as their physical education instructor. We had out-of-state boys there, and I was like the dad of the dorm.

There was a lovely woman who worked in the office, and Deloris and I quickly became friends because we spent a lot of time together on the job.

We started dating. It was great for me because I wasn't looking for a wife, and she wasn't looking for a husband. I felt safe in this relationship. It was so different because

THE BLACK SHEEP

neither of us was looking for romance. She had shared with me that she had been married and divorced. Her husband was chronically unfaithful to her, and finally, she had had enough.

We had been dating six to eight months when she asked me to kiss her. I never would have done that on my own. It felt so strange, but I did it.

A mutual friend of ours sat us down one day. "Look. You two love each other. You should get married."

"No. Not after what my kids have gone through in my previous marriages. I won't subject them to that again. And I have to have a house. And it has to be paid for. Everything needs to be stable."

Deloris and our friend didn't buy that. It was a Tuesday night when they convinced me to get married, and the following Saturday, we said "I do."

Deloris had been raised in Mississippi in a little house in the middle of a cotton field. Hers was a devout family that believed people should live a godly life. Her father was an evangelist, and he preached at revivals. She would play the piano behind him when he was preaching. Now I preach, and she plays the piano behind me.

God sent someone into my life who had been raised totally different. It was very important to me to take Deloris to meet my parents. They hadn't seen or heard from me for a couple of years. All of a sudden one day, there I was, on their doorstep.

When my mom opened the door, it was written all over her face. "Here we go again. Another woman." I

I Will Not Go Quietly

couldn't blame my parents. Every relationship in my life had been a failure. Why should this one be any different? But my wife won their hearts. She was so loving and gracious. If it wasn't for her and how God used her in my life, things would not have turned out so well in the end. She has been and is a major influence in rebuilding my self-esteem. I don't believe I could have become a pastor or the man I am today without her.

It had been 10 years since I had seen my kids by my second wife. She didn't allow visitations. The kids decided they wanted to see me, and they were now old enough to make their demands and were determined to know their dad. They were allowed to call, and I went to pick them up.

When they saw where Deloris and I were living and learned what I was doing, they were just blown away.

"We thought you were a redneck barroom brawler!"

When they learned I had been an assistant pastor at a church in Tennessee and owned my own construction company, they just couldn't believe it.

A few years down the road, my father fell and broke his hip, and he was put in a rest home. When I found out about this, I called him right away. The minute I started talking to him, he started crying. "Son, can you come get me? I don't want to die in a rest home."

Deloris and I packed up and went to Ohio to get both Mom and Dad. We brought them back to Tennessee to live with us.

Since I was involved in setting up the tent revivals, one

THE BLACK SHEEP

night I decided to take my dad. He was about 73 years old at the time. He accepted Jesus as his savior at the revival. It was a miracle!

While I was assistant pastor at a small church, I also worked in construction. The church couldn't afford to pay me a wage. The job site was 60 miles out of town, and there were no phones around.

My mother suddenly became ill. Her intestines some-how got twisted up, and she needed emergency surgery. She sent for me. "Don't touch me until my son gets here!"

They had to drive out and find me on the job. Frantic-ally, I called every minister I knew and asked if they would go to the hospital. Every one of them did. For years, I had prayed that both Mom and Dad would accept Christ. Mom saw the transformation in my life and how my present wife acted in comparison to the past, but I thought if she was ever going to get saved, someone besides me would show her the way because I wasn't "good enough."

When I arrived at the hospital, I didn't give one of my minister friends a chance. Walking up to her bedside, I could see she was visibly shaken and upset. Without a moment's hesitation, I took her hand in mine and said, "Mom, if anything were to happen to you, would you want to know for sure you will go to heaven?"

"Yes."

"Can we pray?"

In that hospital room, holding her hand, I led my mother to salvation. The tears that ran down my cheeks were tears of thanksgiving. My mother had been saved, and I had experienced another major healing in the process. It was such a miracle that the Lord used me, the black sheep, to guide both my parents to salvation.

She made it through the surgery, and there was an incredible change in her life for the year that she lived after that. She gave up drinking and smoking, and her attitude drastically changed. She died at age 67. My dad lived a couple of years after that.

How do you explain a vision, especially to someone who doesn't know God? About two years after my dad died, I had a vision. My parents were standing together, holding hands, in heaven. They waved to me. "Thank you, Tristan." Tears streamed down my face as I realized my parents had finally accepted me, that I had done something right for them.

I thank God that today my relationship with all my children is very good. My oldest son is married and has one child. The second oldest boy just graduated from Missouri Southern with two degrees in criminal justice. He would like to be a parole officer. My third son is in construction. He and my daughter both are married and have great families. I have also been blessed with a stepdaughter who's as wonderful as her mother. She is also married and has a family. All these great kids have made me a grandfather — nine times! Deloris and I have been married for 21 years and have the most wonderful relationship.

My heart is full to overflowing, and I am moved to conclude my story in this way: I met a man named Daren who encouraged me to give my testimony. He believed my

THE BLACK SHEEP

story was powerful because of the things I had experienced in my life.

In the telling of my story, my heart urges me to share with you the tremendous compassion I have for people with afflictions. Those who have physical ones are obvious to us because we can see them. But there are others, those who carry tremendous scars on the inside, where they can't be seen.

Just a few months ago, God gave me tremendous insight into 2 Timothy 2:24-26:

And the servant of the Lord must not strive; but be gentle unto all men, apt to teach, patient, in meekness instructing those that oppose themselves; if God peradventure will give them repentance to the acknowledging of the truth; and that they may recover themselves out of the snare of the devil, who are taken captive by him at his will.

There have been times when I have felt people rejecting me or my preaching, but that's okay now. This scripture has finished the healing in my heart. It's not so much that they are opposing the Bible or me as they are opposing themselves. We sabotage and hide from ourselves. Often I ask myself, "What have they gone through? What's the real deal here?" They are hiding from themselves.

The saving and healing power of Jesus is miraculous. He has totally changed my life and enables me to use my own bad experiences to reach out to others. To this day, I still deal with low self-esteem issues when someone says something thoughtless or negative, but I am healed to where I can take that and overwhelming compassion takes

I WILL NOT GO QUIETLY

over. My heart goes out to them — those who are hurting, who have failed.

As a child, no one but Harold believed in me. I don't blame my parents or anyone else for all my bad decisions. I made them myself. The black sheep is validated and accepted. Jesus Christ is the reason.

As a pastor, I need to tell you that no matter what you have been through, no matter how discouraged you are, don't ever give up on yourself. Seek the Lord and he will heal you, just as he has healed me. Invite Jesus into your heart. When he stretched out his arms on that old rugged cross, he had you in mind. He forgives and heals everything. He will restore your life.

Conclusion

We sincerely hope you have enjoyed these true life stories. But these are not just stories of people who held on with aimless hope. They are people who, through faith in Jesus Christ, have overcome seemingly hopeless situations, not merely surviving, but thriving and overcoming the extreme by God's grace. We invite you to visit Covenant House Christian Center and meet the people whose stories you have read. Come and meet many more people who have similar stories. Covenant House is an exciting church dedicated to the family. We are committed to providing a place where the hurting, depressed and confused can find help, hope, love, guidance, friendship, forgiveness and acceptance, as we provide encouragement and teach Biblical values.

We would love for you to join us on Sunday morning. We gather at 12517 Hartford Avenue, Orofino, Idaho 83544.

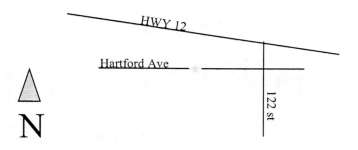

Please call us at (208)476-3803 for directions or contact us at: covenanthouse@orofino-id.com